SEX IS MY BUSINESS

by

CHARLES NUETZEL

WRITING AS "JOHN DAVIDSON"

The Borgo Press
An Imprint of Wildside Press

MMVII

CONTENTS

INTRODUCTION

Small Town USA has been picked on and torn apart, rendered low-class, snobby, closed, narrow-minded, sometimes religiously conservative, and sometimes called Hicksville by the city folk that look down upon them.

I've done my subtle—and not so subtle—knocking at the edges of these types of closed societies. I've let some of my characters rave and rant about Small Town, USA, as they did in *One Summer of Happiness*.

In this book I offer a different view on middle America. It takes place in a town filled with social climbers.

Originally this story was left half-complete in my files, then one day I got a phone call from a publisher wanting a book, and remembered this one, pulled it out, and found myself captured and intrigued. It was all fresh now in my mind. I really wanted to find out what happened next. A prime quality of any story: the desire it inspires in the reader to move to the next scene in an effort to learn more about the characters and conflict and mystery of it all.

Ah, this was going to be fun to complete, I realized.

I had as a central character James Haden, who is

trying to make it in Kilman Enterprises, run by the man who all but owns the town. People are willing to sell themselves out to the highest bidder, and if necessary seduce those in power to help them up the ladder. Even marriages are calculated career makers. The only place love had in their lives was the power it brought into their hands.

And somebody is willing to do anything necessary to protect their own slice of success, even, perhaps, commit murder!

That's the background. The complication that starts things out is the discovery of the dead body in the Kilman home. It is a shock that shoots through the town like wildfire.

The police suspect fowl play, and only the police are able to sort things out.

Against this background James Haden is in love with and determined to marry his boss' daughter, Janet Kilman. This budding romance is suspect, not only by her father, but everybody else involved. But other power players have their take on this matter and their own counter-plans.

The company manager, Gordon Fuller, for one, wants Janet for himself.

And the boss' new young bride, Irene, is determined to keep her place secured at all cost. And at the same time make a play for James as a lover. She had married to gain social status and power, and made no effort to hide that reality to anybody that got in her way. Ol' Man Kilman had wanted a young woman, and she made her deal to be his toy-bride. And nobody dared to challenge that position. She was a very powerful player all on her own, and needed to be catered to on her terms.

Sex is My Business exposes some of the wicked and damnable things people will do to get to the top—and stay there!

—CHARLES NUETZEL
Thousand Oaks, California
August 2006

SEX IS MY BUSINESS, BY CHARLES NUETZEL

CHAPTER ONE

The room was only dimly lit by the pale moonlight, coming through the windows. It caused a soft glow to outline the two nude figures on the bed in the corner.

"You know, I shouldn't really be spending so much time with you, Jimmy," the woman's voice murmured softly, as she clutched tighter to the man. She was only half-serious; and they both knew it. Their little game was just a kind of seductive dance. Neither was serious about one another. They were too ambitious about clawing their way up in the world. "But you sure good for a girl like me! Even then..."

"Why not, Connie?" he asked in a low voice.

Connie snickered softly and then turned her lips up to his. "We're two of a kind. And sure you're one step above me. And I'm just a secretary, right now and...well..."

Connie stared at him and then took a slow, deep drag of her cigarette. "You know that Gordon Fuller is after your neck?"

"Naturally!"

"What are you going to do about it?"

"Nothing—right now." He caressed Connie's fingers. "Don't you worry your little head about that. Old Man Kilman and I are long-time friends, and Gordon can't do anything against me—directly, at least—without Henry Kilman's okay."

Connie's eyes flinched for a moment and then she said: "That *Irene!* She surely cut in big when she married the boss." Her voice had an edge of bitterness to it. "I could almost hate that woman!"

"So she married the man for money—what difference does it make?" Haden asked, sliding his arm around Connie's naked shoulders and pulling her closer to him.

"Just that I'm jealous!" she sighed, putting out her cigarette and turning toward him. She laughed, then said, rather honestly: "I'm willing to do that kind of thing with the right man."

"Well," he teased. "There's Bob, the ol' man's son!"

"A nice, charming young man," she offered, in a serious voice. "I suppose so."

"Bob's very nice. A bit of an idealist, though," he noted.

"Yes. But very nice. Yes, I suppose I could try bagging him. If he'd just notice me. Why don't you fix me up?"

"I might just do that, if you're serious."

She laughed at that. "But then I'd be second best, under Irene, the holy mistress of this small town! If you get my meaning!"

"But that would make you second best!" he pointed out.

"Better that than nothing," she shrugged. "Well, it's that or going elsewhere."

"And why pick up stakes if you can get a good roll right here at home?"

10

She thought for a moment then asked: "And whom are you planning on hunting?"

"I'll never tell. A secret."

"See, we're both alike," she countered.

"And what about love?"

"What about it? What's love got to do with all this?"

"I suppose you're right, in a way. We're all trying to get ahead—"

"And don't care how we do it, just so we win? Right?" she admitted. "I don't mean to be a secretary all my life."

"Not planning on getting married? Having children?"

"To the right guy. With enough bucks to make it worth settling down with him. If you get my meaning."

"And that would be…?"

"Well, somebody will come along!"

"You've been thick with Dale, I've noted."

"Oh, that!" she laughed nervously. "He's just… some guy…nice, sure. But no Bob Kilman. And if I have to pick somebody it would be him. Of course!"

"Then who do you have your claws out for?"

"Well, not with you! If that's what you're worried about. You're as bad as the rest of us. Sex is our business. Not love. And in the long run, sex is a matter of serious *business*, when it opens new doors. And I'm smart enough to play it…smart! If you know what I mean."

"You're hot enough, that's for sure!"

"And I play it dirty with the right partner."

"Like me?"

"Like you, but well, we're kicks! Now aren't

we? An easy Saturday, Sunday through Friday fix between more serious connections! Handy for both of us."

They both laughed at that.

He said: "I suppose you're right. We sell ourselves for the best possible position. Climbing our way up the social ladder."

"It can be fun," she offered, reaching down between them to caress him. "Now can't it?"

"Yes. It can." He admitted thinking about Janet Kilman, whom he planned on bagging, just as Irene had seduced her way into the ol' man's bed to become mistress of the Kilman Kingdom.

Connie said: "We are good together, aren't we?"

"Good for this kind of action, for sure. And you're a great secretary, to boot."

"Not for any longer than I have to be!"

"And I thought you were going to pair up with Dale Robbins!"

"Oh, he's just a kid. Nice, but...well..." She avoided his eyes, then suddenly said: "Oh let's stop all the talking. Just kiss me!"

He didn't need a second invitation. Their lips met eagerly. She trembled against him, as her hands continued exploring his body.

One thing that he could say about Connie, she knew how to please a man, he thought happily. A good secretary to have around until she found another, bigger exec to play games under.

Connie was ambitious and, like she said, willing to bed her way up into power. And he was merrily the first step in the long climb she had set for herself. Like many women in her position they thought it was an original move—sadly it was all too com-

12

mon. Though in her case, she might get very far with her sexual skills and body.

But that didn't make much difference, because he had plans for *himself*.

The form of Janet Kilman took shape before his eyes. Janet, blonde, beautiful, and virginal. The daughter of Old Man Kilman, and the woman he planned on marrying. One way or the other.

Connie's physical actions brought his attention back to her searching hands and lips and the excitement of her body against his.

It was a savage world they lived in; everybody giving their bodies for the price of power and money, but he didn't care much about that, right then.

Suddenly their bodies joined, desperately, thrusting through the last convulsions of ecstasy, and then finally relaxed, exhausted and satisfied.

* * * * * * *

Irene Kilman laughed loudly, downing the drink and then turning her green eyes savagely toward Bob, her stepson. He was going to be so easy to control; literally child's play. It was obvious what the young man wanted, even if he wasn't about to admit it to himself. She could read men so easily. He was jealous and just hurting with desire. It was almost laughable.

"What are you going to do about it?" she taunted nastily, deciding to enjoy a little game-playing. "Tell ol' daddy boy?"

Bob Kilman turned his deep-set eyes on Irene, moving them up and down her tall, beautiful figure.

She was wearing a dark red dress that squeezed every delicious line of her body, revealing, at the low neckline, full, well-shaped breasts.

"You're a cheap little whore!" he remarked in an even, emotionless voice. "You know it and so does everybody else."

"I'm not cheap."

"You slut!" he spit out.

That was one word that hit hard, deep. She hated that.

Irene's face went white and her hand stashed out across the man's face, twisting his head to one side. It happened without thought, instinctively.

"That doesn't change it!" he told her, flatly. "You're just a little scheming tramp. You married dad for money—that's bad enough. But this thing about the other men—that's going too far!"

"What are you going to do about it?" she repeated her voice high-pitched, her breath shortening.

"Tell Dad. That's all there is to do!"

"I wouldn't do that, if I were you!" she snapped, taking a threatening step forward. "I wouldn't do it at all—if you care about living your soft life around here!"

Bob's features froze, becoming tight and set. "This house, everything that dad owns, you're taking—holding. But you can't disgrace him. That's going too far!"

"Nobody knows about it—except you and the men involved!" she pointed out; her expression changed slightly, to become cunning. "Why bother him with such boring details. He's happy enjoying my body. I let him believe I'm madly in love....

14

Power wants the best toys to play with; and I'm number one! He isn't an innocent little boy, like you! Maybe he accepts it all as a lovely fantasy. What he might truly know, somewhere deep in side, well…that can't be helped. Like I said, he isn't foolish. But human. And…powerful! Why ruin things? Let him enjoy the illusion. I'm good at selling that to…any man! He doesn't know what he doesn't want to know…if you get my meaning!"

"And I wouldn't know unless…unless I was just a little smarter than you!"

"Just how *did* you find out?" she asked, softly. The look in her eyes became a little softer, and her lips were just on the verge of smiling tauntingly.

"It wasn't so hard. Once I started wondering what you were doing evenings, I just followed you. Later I had a detective check out on your side activities."

"Very, very clever of you," Irene snapped, her hands clawing unconsciously. With strong control she managed to relax, and then a smile spread across her features. There was a better way to deal with this young man. "But why should we be arguing?"

"What?" surprise showed on Bob's face.

"I mean—I've always *liked* you a lot, Bob. We *could* make some arrangements. You know. Something very private and…well, it could sure be fun!"

The man didn't answer, he only stared blankly at her, and then shock finally made his face turn white.

"You have to admit you think I'm hot. I've seen it! I can read a man's face, his desires are mapped there. You can't keep your eyes off my bod! So don't play that crap in my face!"

She stepped forward, stopping only inches from him. Their bodies were almost touching. "We might—just go together...some place. Alone? I could fulfill all your fantasies about me. You could really discover what you daddy enjoys toying with...what his power and money has bought! Now, be honest, wouldn't you just love to know all those lovely little secrets?"

"You damned slut!" Bob choked out, his face becoming tense and hard. Before he could do anything, Irene slipped her arms around his neck and pulled her body flush with his.

"Come on, you hard young man," she taunted, "You know you want me. I can feel it. And you're so firm and strong...any woman would get hot all over just thinking about you. Honest. I've wondered. We don't have to be enemies. We can be real good friends. The kind that have wonderful secrets to share with each other. Don't be a drag. Just think how much fun we can have. Together. Intimate joys. And I'm very, very good at making a man enjoy...in ways he never could imagine. And I know you want me, Bob. So let's go up to my bedroom!" She felt him tense and then relax against her. His face seemed to soften.

Irene let her lips brush against his, and that was the spark that set his animal desires off balance. Then she pressed her mouth firmly to his and pulled herself tighter against Bob, who was by now desperately returning the kiss, his own lips hungrily crushing to hers.

"You little tramp!" he murmured a moment later, as she moved away, taking his hand and lead-

16

ing him up toward her bedroom. But the deep rasp of overwhelming desire colored those three words.

* * * * * * *

The policeman looked first at Irene and then at her stepdaughter. "You say you discovered the body last night?' he asked, turning his attention toward the younger blonde girl, Janet.

"Yes...it...was..." her tortured voice choked at the words.

It had been horrible for her. Bob Kilman, her brother, killing himself. She couldn't think of a reason in the world for that happening. He had been happy, and with a good future. There wasn't anything he wanted or needed that he couldn't have.

"What could have caused him to do such a thing?"

Irene answered that: "A lot of things. Nobody can go through life without *some* problems. Even us rich people. We're still human. And maybe being rich makes the difference. You get to the point where you can have anything you want and—well, when something goes wrong, you crack! You don't know how to deal."

Just then Lieutenant Brown and Henry Kilman, the Old Man, stepped into the room.

Henry Kilman was white-faced, and the expression in his eyes was almost as dead as his son's.

Lt. Brown said: "We've checked out everything. There doesn't seem to be any doubt that it was suicide. But we'll check it out more completely, just to be sure."

"What!" Irene cried, her face flaring in anger.

"You don't think he was killed? Murdered?"

"Not at all. Just a routine measure. In a case like this it's just normal...well, put it this way: From all indications, many sudden deaths seem like suicide, and then they turn out to be murder. If we didn't investigate all possibilities, a lot of murderers would get off free as birds."

"Oh," Irene sighed. Her face relaxed slightly. "It's just that I can't see any reason why any of *us* would have done it. After all, Bob was a...well, everybody liked him, and there doesn't seem any reason for him to...well, who could have had a reason to *murder* him?"

"I doubt if anybody, Mrs. Kilman. But we'll check it through."

The lieutenant was just turning to leave, motioning the police officer to follow him, when James Haden rushed into the room.

"I just heard about it!" he exploded anxiously. "It can't be true."

"It is," Henry Kilman announced in a flat voice. "He was found in his room with a bullet hole in the side of his head. Quite dead."

"Oh, God, how horrible!" Haden cried, his face becoming stony. *"Why?* Why in the world would he..."

Lt. Brown smiled. "That's what we all would like to know." He turned to Mr. Kilman and announced, "I'll let you know what we find out the moment I get the reports."

"Thank you."

The police left and then Henry Kilman motioned to his wife and they stepped from the room.

James Haden looked at Janet and then moved to

her.

"You poor dear," he said in a low, soft voice, putting his arm around her.

"Oh, don't...don't give me pity!" she half choked out, looking anguished. "Oh, Jimmy, if I didn't have somebody like you. I don't know what I'd do!"

"Okay, let's go!" he urged, kissing her cheek tenderly.

Janet smiled slightly, and then taking his hand in hers, started for the door.

SEX IS MY BUSINESS, BY CHARLES NUETZEL

CHAPTER TWO

The last days had been hectic, but the funeral was now over and James Haden was relieved to be done with that business. Driving home from he cemetery was somewhat depressing to him.

It was late in the afternoon by the time he got back to his apartment. The company had been given a couple of days off in honor of Bob's death. There was a feeling of gloominess running through him, and he couldn't get it out of his mind. He never liked funerals; seemed to him that the people in that business were out to profit on the grief of surviving members of the family. He would never get used to it. To him such events were depressing; not uplifting. It seemed that if one needed to grieve over dear friend of relative, they should do it in private, and not make a public display of those feelings.

Some people considered him a bit weird and uncaring. He was simply private over such matters; and didn't feel comfortable dealing with them. Life was for the living; not the dead.

But there was the subtle mystery as to how Bob had died. Was it murder? Could that be possible? Who could have killed Bob? It didn't make sense. Nor did the young man's death, period. Bob Kilman had been a man whose future was all but perfectly set out for him. And women like Connie Gales had been very interested in bagging him as a husband.

What a waste!

Unlike James Haden, Bob had been born into success, riches, status. All handed down to him by an accident of birth. That was something to celebrate, not kill himself over.

Haden tried to get his mind off of the depressive events of the morning. Off the Kilman family.

The haunting image of Connie Gales suddenly focused in his mind. She was good escape for late at night hours in bed; in fact, any time. No demands, no strings. Just fun and games. They enjoyed each other.

Janet would be needing support, not seductive plays. Socially she was non-touchable at this time.

Haden called Connie but there wasn't any answer. He didn't want to be alone. He called a couple of other women he knew, but that panned out to zero. The only other thing for him was to get be alone or go out and pick up some woman.

He didn't feel like being alone.

He had always been skilled at finding women to take home. Women enjoyed his company. And he needed somebody to take the bitter depressive mood and crush it away. A soft, loving woman's body would focus his mind to more enjoyable sensations.

* * * * * * *

With the funeral done with, now two days in the past, Lieutenant Brown stared at the report that had been handed him concerning Bob Kilman's death. His face expressionless.

"I don't like it," he told the officer standing in front of his desk; it was the same officer who had gone to the Kilman home. "You know, regardless of everything, I can't get the idea out of my mind that this was murder, regardless of the reports!"

"What can you do about it, sir?" the other man asked.

"I don't know. Just don't know. A gut feeling doesn't always work. But there's something more to this than what's in the reports or in the statements the family made. I've got that old gut feeling that it smells."

Brown laid down the report file and said, "Look at it this way: Bob Kilman had everything to live for. No suicide note. No motive. Just a plain killing, which looked in every way like he killed himself. It's too pat. Too complete. And yet there isn't any motive."

Brown's fists slammed down on the table and he compressed his lips across his large teeth. "You know, I can't help thinking it was murder! Regardless! Everything points to suicide. Everything except something inside my mind that won't add up."

"What are we going to do about it?"

"Something. Maybe I'm sticking my neck out. If it weren't for the fact that Henry Kilman runs this damned town, it would be so much easier."

"I should think, sir, Henry Kilman would want you to continue the investigation. After all, he should want the killer found…assuming you're right."

"Can't tell about these rich folks. They're different from you and me. And he's powerful enough to…well, in some ways he owns a big slice of this town and the political seats of power. They all owe him favors. If he wants an investigation of his son, it'll take place. If he doesn't...well that would be it!"

Determination showed on Lieutenant Brown's face and he stood, pushing the chair back. "I'm going to do a little nosing around! We'll see where that leads us."

CHAPTER THREE

It had been some weeks since the funeral.

Henry Kilman and Irene, his wife, were sitting in the small, but comfortable den. The depressive mood of his son's death had been crushing. Still, after the past weeks of shock and pain, the horror still lingered. But it was time to dull all that; to attempt to focus on more immediate issues.

Henry Kilman looked at Irene as she sat before the fire, sipping brandy. He couldn't help thinking how lucky he was to have such a young and beautiful wife. She was his third wife; and he wasn't fool enough to think she hadn't married him for money. To believe otherwise would be rather ridiculous for a man of his age and business sense. He hadn't married her for romantic love. It was, in most respects, a business arrangement; she got what she wanted and paid by giving him what he most desired. And there were many women like, her; but she had been at the right place at the right time and now was his to enjoy. It was calculating and maybe cold-blooded, but that's the way his mind worked.

He'd married her because she had a great body and was simply fantastic in bed. She was a toy-bride, a plaything for a rich, successful man; she looked the part and acted the part, and was a lady in

25

the parlor and a whore at night in bed. The last years of his life were being made into a wonderful time of pleasure—all because of Irene's attention to him. Nothing, really, mattered beyond that—once the company's future was resolved. Then he planned on traveling and making the best used of the years ahead.

Life was too short to focus on hellish issues. His first wife had died of cancer at an early age and his second had been a nice, respectable lady, but not too great in the bedroom, so he'd fashioned a life with several ladies on the side. Divorce was threatened when his wife discovered his extra-marital affairs. But before things had been legally resolved she'd been killed in an auto accident brought on by driving when drunk. In the last years of their marriage she'd been drinking far too much.

Then a number of other women passed through his life after that. He made use of those that offered their bodies for his favors. Most were simply useful toys for a short time. His latest marriage was special in that Irene offered what he needed on several levels as a model wife.

He wanted to enjoy their life together; and nothing could stand in the way of that.

The death of his son was something that needed to be crushed into some back burner, hidden away; it couldn't destroy what was still good about life.

Too many people let the death of a child ruin their lives. And he wasn't about to let that happened. Plus he had a daughter to care about—that has to come first. It was simply a matter of re-shifting his gears. No son to take over the business; so Janet had to be matched with the right man who would handle company business in a realistic and skillful way. Finding a possible son-in-law would be far more important than grieving over something that couldn't be changed.

After all, death was simply a part of the living experience; even if an ending. And that came far too soon for everybody.

He was, if nothing more, a practical man who had survived and built a company that pretty much owned and ran the town. *The Kilman Empire*, as he considered it, was far more important than the life of any one person—even if it was his son.

He had more important matters to contend with. His own life to life. That might be cold, uncaring, but that's the way his mind worked.

He had met Irene when she worked for his company, at an office party, and the way she'd gone out of her way to play up to him had left no doubt in his mind that here was a woman willing to do anything for money and position. And he'd played it for all it was worth. Even against his son's warning that he was stepping into one hell of a trap.

Thought of his son knotted a hardness in his throat.

Why? Why would Bob kill himself? Kilman had asked himself that question over and over and hadn't gotten the answer.

He wanted to shut that off. Stop thinking about his son's loss. It was time for put that in the past.

The loss of a child was a terrible thing to experience. He would never get past that, really. But the time of self-indulging grieving had to come to an end.

Sighing heavily, Henry Kilman took a slow

swallow of brandy from the glass in his hand. The warmth of the liquor moved through his system and numbed the bitterness inside his mind and soul, for the time being, at least.

"Irene," he said, looking at his wife again.

She turned her head in his direction. "Yes?"

"How about an evening out?"

"That'd be wonderful! I think it is about time we rejoined the world."

"Yes. I think you're right. It would do some good. I don't like sitting here and just thinking about—well, about Bob. He's gone and buried. We have to let him rest right there in the ground. Go on with our lives. Right?"

"Right!" she agreed.

"There's no point to just stop living. And I won't act up some false socially accepted grief period...I won't just sit here hiding away. The public be damned. I'll go nuts here. What Bob did was foolish. That's it. He...never mind. I don't want to think about him. We have to keep on. And sitting here doesn't help matters any."

"You're a dear. I agree, time to join the world," she said in a tender sounding voice. "I'll go get dressed."

"And not in black. We're not going to fall into that year of grief...running around in black. If the townspeople don't like it, tough. If the social upper class don't approve...well, I won't do business with them any more!"

She laughed at that. "And they can't afford to lose your support, my dear husband."

His wife was a good actress; and a smart woman. She knew how to deal with the reality of

Henry Kilman.

"How about the country club?" he suggested. "Or anywhere you want.

"Okay, then. The whole town, high to low."

* * * * * * *

"Time to live!" Connie Gales told herself as she looked in the minor. All her fancy plans about getting to know Bob Kilman had been shattered. Now all she could do was make the best of things. Continue to play secretary and make the necessary connections with young men at the office. Now was a time for waiting things out until she found the right guy to play up to. Connie didn't expect to remain a sectary all her life. She had plans!

She had a date with a young man in the office; the only man she cared anything about, really, outside of her boss, James Haden. With him it was business. She'd marry him in a flash if he was open to such an idea. But the man was driven like many people, and out to climb upwards through marriage, not downwards. She was something he enjoyed for momentary pleasure. Connie was smart enough to understand that; and accept it realistically. Somebody would come into her future life to fulfill her personal needs. But for now this young man was a nice distraction; and she really liked him. Under other circumstances he might even seem like a neat life-partner. But that was not in her plans. He wasn't a stop upwards on the social latter; just a nice dating friend.

The doorbell rang and she fluffed up her hair to make it look a little casual, almost wind-blown, then

29

turned and went across the small living room.

"'Hi, Dale," she said as she flung the door open.

The tall, dark-haired man rushed in and swept Connie into his arms.

"It's been a long lime!" he breathed.

She felt a nervous giggle move through her. "Dale Robbins, you act like you haven't seen me in weeks!"

"I haven't!" he told her, moving across the room to where a small cabinet stood. "Not since the funeral, to be exact! And that's weeks!"

Dale fixed two highballs and then moved to the sofa, sitting down and patting the cushion next to his. Connie accepted the open invitation and settled herself next to Dale.

He handed her one of the highballs and then said, "I don't like all this night work you're doing with Mr. Haden!"

For a moment Connie had the terrible feeling that he had guessed exactly what that "night work" was. And the arrangement with Jim was pretty basic. They understood one another.

But one look into Dale's still youthful and innocent eyes, and she realized it was quite impossible for him to even imagine she would ever do such a thing as enjoy a very racy, casual sexual affair with her boss. After all, he was in love, and she could pretty well guess that it was probably his first real love. That was rather charming, in a way.

As for herself, she really didn't know exactly how she felt toward Dale. There was a very strong sexual attraction between them, but she had no way of knowing, as yet, if it actually went any further than mere sex. Of course, he didn't fit into her future plans—other than a nice romantic connection from time to time. He was nice company. And a real friend. Which was nice, as far as that went.

They had met some months before, and the dating had started out casually. Nothing serious, on her part, only sex. She needed men around to keep the lonely nights from being a hell. Even Jim Haden didn't take up all her time, nor fill all her needs. She hated being alone.

The fact was, she had developed a need to have Dale around. In a way he was being used. She couldn't, even if she wanted to, cut him out of her life—not right at this time, anyway. Bottom line: he was fun and games. And that was, for sure, better than being alone. Life was too short to toss away.

"What's with you, Connie?" Dale asked, patting her thigh. "You've been sitting there thinking and thinking, and not even listening to what I was saying."

"Oh, I'm sorry. What were we talking about?" she asked, turning and smiling at Dale. His lean features relaxed and he smiled back warmly.

Quickly she thought, then lied: "It wasn't really so important. We were talking about Bob Kilman's death this afternoon at work. You know Bob Kilman? The investigation over his...death. Some people think it might be murder."

"Oh, everybody wants to make a big mystery out such things," he stated, with a shrug. "It's been weeks, now."

"I know, but everybody at the company and in town is caught up in the mystery and intrigue of the whole thing."

"Isn't that normal? Everybody knew Bob. Everybody knows the Kilman family, directly or indirectly. We all are supported by the company, one way or the other. It keeps the town running and healthy."

"Sure…who doesn't in this town?" she asked, a little surprised at his question.

"The police are investigating, but they say he killed himself. I think that's what happened."

"But why?" she wondered. "That's what everybody wonders."

"Let the police work it all out. As for me, I don't really care all that much. The first week or so, it was interesting news. Now…time to get on with other things! Like tonight. You and me."

But she couldn't get her mind off the puzzle of Bob Kilman's sudden death. It didn't seem possible that Bob could have any reason to kill himself. She knew the general facts about the Kilman household, as everybody else who worked for Kilman Enterprises did—and maybe a little more.

Bob had lived a life of fun—and nothing much more. When Irene had married his father it had been rumored he'd blown his top, for several reasons.

One: they claimed he had had his eye on Irene.

Two: that Irene was too young for his father. And no doubt there were countless other reasons. But the fact that there had been conflict between Bob and Irene didn't add up to any reason for him to kill himself.

"There you go again—thinking!"

"I'm sorry, Dale. Time to have some fun and stop thinking about this I have no control over."

"Great. About time. You know how I feel about you…and…well…"

"Okay, down the drinks and let's get going! Fly me to the moon and back!"

* * * * * * *

James Haden looked sorrowfully into his martini, and then after a moment he gulped the contents and ordered another. He'd been in the bar for over an hour, and nothing had come in. No woman worth the effort it would take to woo and bring to his apartment.

The martini came and he stared numbly at it for a moment and then took several swallows. The band around his head began to tighten.

Haden turned his eyes toward the mirror behind the counter and looked over the customers in the place. There were a couple of girls—women in their late twenties—sitting at a table. They were fairly attractive, but from the look of their dresses and the way they giggled to each other, he was pretty sure they were a dead end. Women coming together could be a problem. He liked it better when a woman walked in alone and made it obvious she was interested in being picked up. When they came with somebody they tended to be more interested in just having fun there, not going elsewhere. At least, that was his attitude.

He returned his attention to the glass, and then after a couple of seconds looked back at the mirror.

Surprise jolted through him.

Connie Gales and a young man who worked at the office were just sitting down at a table. For only a moment did Haden hesitate and then, deciding, he stood up from the bar stool and moved over to

33

where Connie was sitting.

"Well, hello, imagine seeing *you* here!" he said, seating himself beside the girl.

Connie looked at him, her face blanching for a moment, and then her eyes took on a slightly annoyed expression.

"Well, hello, Mr. Haden," she greeted in a voice that was too impersonal.

"Come on, what's this Mr. Haden stuff, after what's been between the two of us?"

There was a frozen silence, and then the young man next to Connie glared at Haden and then glanced at Connie.

"Just what does he mean by that?" Dale Robbins asked.

Connie quickly answered. "Oh, nothing. Nothing at all!"

If Haden hadn't been feeling his drinks so much he wouldn't have made his next remark. The words just came out: "I only meant that we were on more than just speaking terms. That's all!"

Suddenly Haden realized what he had said, and quickly added: "Nothing really beyond that—I mean...we've just been out together a few times, that's all."

Dale Robbins stared at Haden for a long moment and then his eyes slowly moved to Connie. "I thought you said it was only work."

"Well, I don't see what difference it really makes," Connie quickly put in. "So what if I go out with other men...?"

"Oh, come on, Connie!" Dale snapped bitterly. "That's not the point! The thing is that you weren't honest with me!"

There was a moment's silence and then Connie turned savagely toward Dale. "I don't see what business it is of yours!"

"Just that I thought you wouldn't do such a thing!"

"Do what?"

"Lie to me!"

"You poor little boy! What do you think life is made up of? Good little boys and good little girls that never, never do anything but tell the truth?"

The drinks came and Dale paid for them. Connie drank down the martini, gulping it, and quickly ordered another before the cocktail girl could leave.

"Don't you think you're taking that a little fast?" Dale asked evenly.

"What's wrong? Don't you have the money?"

Dale's face hardened and his eyes became cold. "What's gotten to you?"

"Just *you!* And your petty little mind!"

"I don't see what's so—"

"Oh, cut it out!" she snapped angrily, glaring at the young man.

Dale turned to Haden and said evenly, "You wouldn't mind leaving us, would you?"

"He'll do nothing of the sort!" Connie cut in, her voice hard and cold.

"Maybe it would be better if I left," Haden suggested.

"You stay!" Connie said in a soft voice, her hand reaching out and taking hold of his. "If Dale-boy here can't stand the competition, then he can...well, he knows what to do about it!"

The second martini came and Connie downed it quickly, ordering a third.

"Connie!" Dale objected. Then turning to the cocktail waitress he said, "I don't think she needs that next one."

Connie quickly snapped, "I'll have that drink!"

"No!" Dale ordered.

The cocktail waitress stood there, not knowing what to do.

Connie turned toward Haden and asked, "Would you buy me a martini?"

For a moment Haden didn't know what to say. He didn't like cutting the other man out, considering the ethics; but on the other hand, he didn't mind the idea of getting Connie away from the younger man who from all outward appearances didn't know how to really handle her.

Dale was the one who settled it. The man stood and looked down at Haden, saying, "You wouldn't mind taking Connie home?"

Connie took in a deep, startled breath, surprised.

"There's no reason for that," Haden remarked, feeling suddenly embarrassed.

"It would seem Connie is more in the mood for *your* company!" Dale said softly, stepping away, walking across the room and then out the door.

"Wait a minute," Haden said to Connie, standing and walking after the other man. Once outside the cocktail lounge, he stepped up to Dale. "Look, this isn't what I want!"

Dale Robbins turned and looked blankly at him. "I know. But there's just so much a man can take. I'm sorry. But...would you mind terribly?"

Haden looked at him for a long moment suddenly aware of the torment the other was going through.

He felt sorry for Robbins, but there wasn't really anything that could be done about it now. The man was still young and innocent. And a damned fool!

No doubt Dale had Connie Gales on a tall pedestal. The damage had been done, and it was all to Haden's benefit. He had wanted to be with Connie that evening, and now he had the opportunity being thrown at him.

He shrugged, actually relieved.

"Okay, sucker!" he said nastily, walking back into the club. A moment later he was sitting next to Connie.

"I'm terribly sorry about this," he told her.

"It really doesn't matter, does it?" Her eyes told him it mattered a lot, but that she wasn't about to admit it to him or anybody else.

Shrugging, he left the question unanswered. "Want that drink?"

"Not really." Connie stared at him for a moment and then said in a low voice: "Take me some place where we can be alone together."

Nodding, he took out his wallet, laid down enough money to cover the bill and stood up. They walked out and then got into his car. A moment later he was heading toward his apartment.

SEX IS MY BUSINESS, BY CHARLES NUETZEL

CHAPTER FOUR

Janet Kilman had lain on her bed for hours, not sleeping, haunted by the nightmare dreams about her brother and his sudden and unexpected death. It still seemed impossible that it could have happened. Bob had been so full of life, so anxious about his future. It had been all spread out for him. Up to the time of his death he'd only played at living, but the prosperous company their father had developed would have gone into his hands. Now…

Now everything was changed. She realized that her father had taken it hard, and she was a little afraid of how it might affect him. He had been numb for weeks, until tonight when he and her Irene had got out.

"Damn it all!" she cursed, sitting up. She couldn't just stay there in her room, feeling sorry for herself and for her brother and her father.

Maybe a drink would help?

A quick fix. And she knew that wasn't the smart answer.

She was bored. That was part of it.

She got up from the bed and walked down to the den, where her father kept the supply of liquor. It was only a matter of minutes before she had finished one double shot of whiskey.

She wished James Haden was there with her. They hadn't seen one another for days. It would have been better just to be with him. The man was a nice date, dinner companion and friend. She realized he probably had romantic ideas about her; that or merely sexual designs. And he seemed to care about her, which was nice, at least. He had a reputation as somewhat of an office playboy. But she realized most single men played it loose and easy with women. She was always shy of men, knowing that a lot would want to court her for her money, position. And now with her brother's death it was even more serious. Whomever she married would probably be running the Kilman Empire. That made her an easy target for fortune hunters. And her father would be watching very closely whom she dated. Still, even then, James Haden was certainly an attractive male in just about every way. At least on the surface. And their fathers had been, apparently, good friends at one time or another.

But she suddenly realized the truth. She was afraid of James Haden. Not of what he might do to her—it wasn't that. But rather or the strong sexual urge she felt toward him. And his ideas of morality.

All her life she had been brought up to believe that sex should be saved for marriage. Now at the age of twenty-five, Janet was beginning to wonder exactly what the whole point was of waiting. What was so valuable about being a virgin? What was she saving it for? Most girls her age had had their share of men, and from what she heard from her friends, it was the only way to fly.

Yet, Janet had managed to keep herself at a safe distance from sexual intimacy. Only once before

40

had she been tempted, and that was the night a boy had given her her first drink. It was the last year of high school and they were out on a date together. He'd done everything but rape her in his attempted seduction. Janet had managed to fend him off.

She was a prude.

Janet poured herself another drink.

You've got to stop using booze, she told herself. Yet liquor helped it make it possible to think more honestly; more brutally.

Maybe the best thing for her was to have a man. For over a year now it had been getting harder and harder to keep to the strict moral attitude.

She was just a stupid fool. About time she grew up. Before it was too late. Her brother had played around. Thank God for that, now that he was dead. Terrible thing to die a virgin! And there was no question about her father. The man had been pretty active throughout his life—having a number of affairs.

Janet decided.

Maybe call Haden. Enough time had passed since they'd seen each other after her brother's death.

She would talk him into coming over. Then things would work themselves work out.

She smiled slightly, wondering if it would be possible to set up a seduction scene with him—or any man, for that matter. Though, she admitted, with Jim it certainly wouldn't be all that difficult; he was known to be experienced at such matters. He'd probably make all the seductive moves on his own; all she had to do was avoid blocking him. No stops!

Walking over to the den phone, she picked up

the receiver and dialed Haden's number. After letting it ring ten times she replaced the receiver, looked at the whiskey glass in her hands and then downed its contents.

Maybe getting a little drunk would help? At least get her past this moment.

What was getting into her? she thought bitterly, walking back to the home bar and pouring another glass of whiskey.

The numbing band around her head was already beginning to dull her thoughts. Sitting down in a chair, she tried to relax and blank out her fuzzy reflections.

She wished Jim Haden had answered the phone.

Many men had wanted her, but she'd put up all the stops.

Janet took another swallow of the whiskey and then closed her eyes. What she needed was a complete blackout.

It seemed that she sat there for a long time, aware of the soothing effects of the liquor. Then slowly the blackness became heavier and darker, and then it started to become alive. Janet didn't really know when reality ended and fantasy began.

She was floating on a blanket of black and dropping downwards, ever downwards into a pit that seemed to open below her.

"You want love! Let me kiss your lips, let me fold your body against mine."

She was aware of the voice and then aware that she recognized it.

James Haden.

A moan broke from her lips and then suddenly changed to a scream. A scream of terror. A scream of fear.

Abruptly Janet's eyes jerked open.

The dream faded quickly into her subconscious. Reality surrounded her. The warmth of the den and the book lined walls.

She stood, shakily and moving to the bar.

Only for a moment was there a mental reserve that repelled from the idea of becoming drunk.

Five minutes later she was walking up to her room, a glass and the bottle of whiskey in her hands.

* * * * * * * *

James Haden awoke with the burn still heating through his body. Connie Gales was lying in bed next to him. Slowly he turned and looked at the girl. It had been quite an evening. They'd come to his apartment, had a few drinks, gotten in the mood by dancing a little to the radio, and then without any actual direct, suggestion, they had stepped into the bedroom undressed and then slide into bed.

Haden looked down at Connie. The sheet was only half covering her breasts, which rose and fell slightly with her breathing. One nipple was red and exposed, peeking omit over the whiteness of the sheet like a little eye calling to him.

He couldn't help feeling a reaction of tenderness toward Connie. She was a sensitive woman, but one who was selling herself for the chance to get ahead. She was playing the tightrope game of giving her body on the chance that the arrangement might advance her career.

And she was one skillful package of joy in bed; she really liked sex. And that was the element that

43

made it possible for her to play that tightrope game more effectively.

His eyes refocused on the erect, rosy eye peeking at him.

Smiling, Haden moved his lips down toward her tempting breast. He would wake her and they'd enjoy delicious wild sex together. She was good at that!

At contact, a moan sounded from Connie's lips. Then suddenly Haden felt her hands claw at the back of his neck, and a surprised intake of breath sounded from her lips.

She pressed his head deeper into her breasts, her body squirming lightly.

Jim Haden knew the weekend was just beginning.

CHAPTER FIVE

Lieutenant Brown sat sipping coffee, trying to get the Monday blues out of his sleepy mind. The month had been filled with frustration for him and he had a lot of thinking to do about it.

He'd done a lot of foot work on his own time, talking to friends and people who knew Bob Kilman. There had been a complete blank-out.

Nobody could think of a reason why Bob Kilman would kill himself.

The picture Brown had built of the man was that of a modern, rich playboy scion whose future was mapped out. Once his father either died or retired, he would have taken over Kilman Enterprises, and then he'd continue cashing checks and not doing anything for the money—unless he wanted to.

Gordon Fuller ran the whole project, and there wasn't any need for the owner to do anything. And from what Brown had learned about Bob Kilman's plans for the future they hadn't included doing any thing but cashing checks every week and boozing and loving it up

He had a long list of girl friends.

There was something else that Brown had learned about Bob Kilman. The man had hired a private detective to get a line on his stepmother.

One interesting fact had come out of that information. Irene Kilman had several men with whom she was having very discrete affairs. From all indications Mrs. Kilman was a woman with an extreme interest in men. Fact: she had married Henry Kilman, an older man. Fact: therefore she had married for money, not for love.

That second fact had been fairly obvious in the beginning, but not proven. Now it could be considered a proven fact.

Conclusion: While having married Henry Kilman for money, she had continued to carry on affairs with other men—and Bob Kilman had found out.

Another fact: Bob Kilman had been known to hate his stepmother.

Where did it fit in?

Lieutenant Brown took another sip of his coffee and looked at the far wall, trying to think. But the thoughts wouldn't organize. They just went around and around.

The facts were simple; but damning. And he couldn't get the case out of his mind. The puzzle continued to plague him.

Bob Kilman had been found dead in his room. Supposedly he had killed himself. But there wasn't any motive—unless you might say that he found out about his stepmother's little side activities, and decided to kill himself.

Interesting idea; but fowl.

Plus Irene Kilman's affairs were public to all who wanted to know.

It just didn't make sense. That wasn't a motive for a man who was having a ball in life. Maybe with a guy who was cracked...

There was one other little bit of information: Bob Kilman had just found out about his step-mother's activities, the very day he was found dead. The detective hired to do the investigation had made his report only that afternoon. Just about two or three hours before Kilman was found dead.

Any connection? Damned right! But the motive?

The Kilman family wanted to get past all this; fast. They wanted to accept the apparent facts. And word had come down to him to keep any investigation very quite and in the background. "Let the family heal!"

* * * * * * *

Monday morning and Haden was suffering a hang-over. The weekend was over and the fun ended. Another week and another possible step up-ward. The weeks were just slipping away from him. Much too fast.

The times with Connie Gales had been reward-ing enough, but hadn't gotten him any place except into the world of escape. But that was what he had needed. Escape.

Escape from the waiting for the right moment when he could and would make his a serious play for Janet Kilman. One way or the other, Jim planned on getting married to her.

He realized that now whoever that might be would be giving the controlling interest in Kilman Enterprises. And that's exactly what he wanted. But there was the factor of Gordon Fuller, who ran things at the moment. And that man would be after Janet's hand in marriage, if he had his brains the right place.

James Haden knew that he had an inside trap, personally, with Janet, but not, necessarily as a future husband. Her father favored him as a friend, though it as difficult to know how the man felt concerning him as a future son-in-law. That was a totally different issue.

He would have to make a serious play for Janet, before it was too late. Timing was a serious factor. Maybe enough time had passed for him to start pressing hard on the lovely young woman.

The time was ripe.

Connie came into his office, all smiles, and said: "Mr. Fuller wants to see you."

"Right away?" he asked, looking up at his secretary.

"Right away!"

"Say what it was?"

"No."

"Keep your fingers crossed then, honey."

Connie smiled warmly, and as he stood and started around the desk, she moved in close to him and placed a gentle kiss on his cheek. "For good luck!"

It took only a few seconds to go across the hall and into Gordon Fuller's office.

The general manager of Kilman Enterprises was a tall, good-looking man with graying temples. From what Haden had learned about Fuller and his activities, the man liked to think of himself as God's gift to women. And, even more important, the God of Kilman Enterprises. He ruled the place with a

48

cold, iron hand. Even if he did have a certain amount of natural charm; and a keep business sense.

Fuller had been trying to get an inside track with Janet Kilman for years, but hadn't gotten much further, from what Haden could tell, than a goodnight kiss and friendship.

But then, James Haden hadn't gotten much further, either.

"Hello, Jim, sit down, I have a few things to talk to you about," Fuller greeted in a flat voice.

They didn't like one another; but got along. Fuller seemed to look on Haden as a lazy, no-good leach, who had gotten his position through connections and not through hard work.

For the most part, that was fairly close to being true—everything except that lazy bit. He'd worked hard from the moment he had been put in charge of government contracts.

"I just thought we should have a talk about how things are…now that Bob is out of the picture. Terrible thing about Bob, but enough time has gone by to put things on the table and be up front as to how the company is going to be run from now on." Fuller stated matter-of-factly.

That man's eyes were as cold as his voice. There was an almost evil feeling about him. He'd worked tirelessly, and had gotten to be top kick the hard way. But he was also a scheming bastard. His gray eyes stared at Haden for a long time in silence. Then he said: "I wish to hell that…well, I'd just as soon not be in this position. But we might as well face realities. Old Man Kilman has made it clear that for the time being he won't be handling matters here—sort of a temporary retirement—which puts me in complete control!"

"Why are you telling me this?" The man had been in control for a very long time. Maybe the only change might be that Kilman was making it official, now that his son was out of the equation.

There was a stony silence, broken by Fuller's next words: "Just to let you know where you stand, now."

"And exactly where do I stand?" Haden asked, trying to sound unconcerned and casual, lighting a cigarette.

"There will be a little change in policy. A little tightening down. And if somebody can't keep up, I'll see what can be done to replace them."

"Oh?"

"I understand you and Janet Kilman have been seeing a lot of each other...I know you have designs in that area."

That was blunt.

"So?"

"Well, a man in your position in the company shouldn't have so much free time to spend on social activities with the boss's daughter. If you get my meaning." Fuller's tone was hard and cold. And the man's attitude was icy hard, cutting to the raw bone. He was not playing games, not being subtle about it. "But that's not what I brought you in here for. I want you to go to Washington. There's this new government contract that you're to see about. Make arrangements for the tying up of that NASA affair—you know all about the deal."

Haden nodded. This was one project very important to the company. He had wanted the assignment.

The next half hour was taken up in covering final details.

Once he left the office, Haden realized exactly where he stood with the other man.

What Fuller had actually communicated by implication, and by direct wording, was that Jim would be kept as busy as possible. If he didn't want to face that possibility, then he would either have to quit the job or drop his relationship with Janet Kilman.

The general manager was afraid of him. And wasn't about to play fair in the courting of Janet Kilman. The man's bluntness had surprised him.

There was something bubbling behind the scenes that Haden didn't know about. Something that Fuller wanted to put an end to and quick.

Haden returned to his office, to study the reports necessary for his assignment in Washington.

Janet he would deal with after his little business trip. Let Fuller play his little game, it wouldn't help in the long run. Janet wasn't a fool; and Fuller wasn't Mr. Charm. The only edge he might have was Ol' Man Kilman's backing as a future son-in-law and Master of the Kilman Enterprises.

The power-play for control of the company had been put into place, and the manager had all the triggers under his nasty fingertips. The only edge Haden might have is if Janet could be convinced he was the shining knight to sweet her off her feet.

But first things first; keep his position at the company rock solid so Fuller couldn't yank the rug out from under him.

SEX IS MY BUSINESS, BY CHARLES NUETZEL

CHAPTER SIX

On the plane to Washington, Haden had a lot of time to think about other matters outside of business. Considerations which had never really occurred to him before.

He had been bumming around all his life, more or less, until he'd landed the soft position at Kilman Enterprises. His father and Henry Kilman had been good friends all their lives, and years before Henry had done everything he could do to get young Jim Haden to take a job with his company, but it had taken over ten years of bumming to come to the point in life where he was willing to face reality.

There had been the five years in the Air Force, becoming a staff sergeant, boozing at the beer joints that usually surrounded airbases, taking up with the broads who were there for a price of a drink or for a few bills for their services in bed.

Then after that there had been a brief affair with a high society lady, who had been married for money to an old guy who'd died and left her with a fortune the two of them had managed to make a big dent.

It had been this period of Haden's life which had given him a taste of what real money and an easy life could mean. That was when his plans to himself set up in such a position had caused him to return home and that Henry Kilman's offer.

Plus the memory of Janet Kilman as a teenage girl. She'd now be in her middle twenties, easy pickings for a man who knew the score.

It was cold-blooded; but realistic.

It had been easy for these first months.

But Bob Kilman's death was changing things, fast. And there was a somewhat puzzling "mystery"—had he been killed? And why? And how did that effect the equations for power?

If somebody had killed Bob, who might it be? Who would profit the most from the man's death?

Gordon Fuller?

The thought intrigued him. Could Fuller have been able to kill for a little more power? If given the chance to get away with it, that was possible. He was a cold-blooded bastard. The man wanted to marry Janet Kilman to safeguard his position in the company. There wasn't anything wrong with that as long as he played the game fair. But Fuller wouldn't play fair.

Angrily, Haden dropped those thoughts. There wasn't anything that he could do about it, now. Not until he returned to Kilman Enterprises.

Think about something different!

Janet...tiny, delicate, and blonde.

He supposed it wouldn't be too hard to fall in love with Janet. But the thing was: in love or not, he would marry her the very next day, if it was possible.

Love simply had nothing to do with it.

Haden had learned to "grab what you can—because if you don't somebody else will."

The morals and ethics be damned. As long as you kept within the law.

Murder was out!

What about Fuller?

Forget Fuller!

The plane flight was dull and uninteresting. Haden did his best to forget everything about the Kilman family. Enough was enough.

In Washington, the business affair went at a normal dull rate, and finally, after a week, Haden had the contracts for doing research on a rocket fuel all signed and sealed. It was in all respects a dull but successful trip.

On arriving back in home, the little community in which Kilman Enterprises ruled with an iron hand, he was weary and looked forward to a few days of rest. He had just arrived at his apartment and was settling down to a quick meal when the telephone rang.

"Yes?"

"Fuller!"

"What's it you want, now?"

"Business!"

"It's five-thirty and I'm just a little tired. And anyway—"

"You're still on business hours!"

"I got the contracts. And if you don't relax and take it easy, I'll shove them down your..."

"There's no need to get mad!" Fuller said in a more silky voice. "That's all I wanted to know. Show up tomorrow..."

"Hell, this is Friday and I'm..."

"Be at my house tomorrow at ten!"

The phone went dead.

Angrily Haden hung up the receiver and was half-way back to his dinner table and meal when it rang again.

He returned to the phone and again picked up the receiver. "Yes?"

"James Haden?" It was a woman's voice. "Yes."

"This is Irene Kilman. I want to see you."

"What?"

"It's important. Can I come over to your place?" He thought that over. *What did Irene want to see him for?* They didn't have anything in common, except the fact that they were both social climbers, willing to sell their bodies for only one purpose: the next step up to an easy life. The only two differences between them were that she was a woman and that she had already made her point. *What the hell did she need him for?*

"Can't we talk about it over the phone?"

"No!"

"I'll meet you some place!"

There was silence to that and then he heard a sigh, followed with: "Okay. How about the...well—no! It wouldn't be a good idea at that. I don't want it to be public—"

"If it's something that—"

"Nothing to worry about. Just private. Can I come up?"

"Okay. Come on up. In about an hour?"

"Fine. I'll see you then."

The receiver clicked.

Puzzled, Haden stepped over to the dinner table and started eating. But his mind wasn't on the food. For some reason he had the feeling that Irene's visit was going to have far-reaching effects. And he

56

didn't like that idea at all. Not at all.

It smelled. There hadn't been much personal relations between Mrs. Kilman and himself since she'd been married.

Before she'd hooked Old Man Kilman, Jim had tried to make a mild pass at her, only because she was an attractive young woman and had a reputation for being easy. It hadn't been blocked, exactly, only put off, because she had another date for the evening. She'd said to try again, sometime. He never had.

The whiskey felt good in his guts, burning some of the tiredness from his body.

He was just standing up to get himself another double shot when the doorbell rang. Haden changed his direction, and a moment later he was closing the door behind Irene Kilman.

He looked at the woman, taking in the full sweep of her body, which was beautifully packaged in a tight-fitting brown dress. The neckline was all the way up, but the tightness of the silken cloth around her pointed breasts seemed to be more openly sensual than if they had been nudely exposed.

Irene smiled and looked at the empty glass in Haden's hand. "You drinking, Jim?"

"Was about to fix myself another."

"Mind if I have one?"

"Sure—all I have is whiskey," he said, trying hard to keep his eyes away from her body.

"That'll be fine."

"Sit down, make yourself at home," Haden directed, moving into the kitchen. In a few moments he returned with two drinks.

Irene Kilman was sitting on the sofa, her right arm laying on the back, her body arranged in such a way that it showed off the beauty of her long legs. She took the drink he handed her without comment. "I guess you're wondering why I wanted to see you."

"You might say that."

After taking a large swallow of the whiskey, Irene looked directly up at him, her eyes meeting his, evenly. "I want to be direct and to the point. I think we owe that much to each other. This is about Janet."

For a moment Haden was taken aback. "What about Janet?"

"You've been seeing a lot of her, and to be honest, I can pretty much see what is going on in your mind."

"I don't know what you're talking about!" Haden said in an evenly controlled voice, continuing to stand and look down at the woman.

"I'll be blunt! You're out to marry Janet—for money! Position, power!"

"Is that a crime in *your* book?"

Irene considered that for a moment and then said, "That all depends."

"On what?"

"Well, let's put it this way." She paused to take another swallow of her drink and then continued, slowly, picking her words with care.

"I'll be frank. No sense in bull shitting you. We're two of a kind. Calculating, and willing to do anything to get what we want. I've gone to a lot of trouble, effort and time...what I mean is that my marriage with Henry wasn't really the romance of the year. I'll admit that. Even if he's a lovely man. But frankly, it was to me a purely business arrangement. I make him happy and I guess that's all that really matters. He gets what he wants from me, and I get what I want. I'm his toy-bride, his show-doll, and hostess and I play the roles like a pro. I'm good at it. We both don't have to be silly and foolish and lie about such matters. I think it is clear we have to be bluntly honest between the two of us. Right?"

He shrugged, deciding to play it close to his chest.

"I don't see where this is leading, Mrs. Kilman!"

"Simply this: *one social climber in the family is enough!*" Her eyes were hard fires, staring deeply into his. "I don't want competition!"

"I don't see where it is any of your business...or rather, what you can do about it!"

"Oh, there is a lot I can do. Don't make that mistake!"

"Are you threatening me?"

"Not really, just feeling you out. The thing is that I can be a lot of good help to the right person— or make things pretty impossible for the wrong person! If you get my meaning, honey, dear!"

Haden stared down at Irene, wondering exactly what the point was. "Okay, you tell me what you have in mind—if nothing else, I must admit I'm a little curious."

"*If* I arrange things so they are easier for you, what...well, put it this way—exactly what is it that you're after? No sense in being coy about it, Jim."

"Why not just say I'm in love with Janet and

want to marry her? She doesn't know it yet, but in time I'll pop the question to her!"

"I can believe *that!"* Irene laughed. "You're a pretty slick operator! You've been around the block a number of times, with some ladies, I've learned. Oh, don't look surprised. A simple call to a detective friend and details are quickly supplied. And I'm not against discovering all the details I need to know about. So...drop the act!"

There was a short silence and then Haden broke it with a question. "Exactly why have you waited this long to...well, to talk about this with me?"

"Bob's death puts things in a different light. Janet will be inheriting the business. With a smart operator like yourself...but maybe I shouldn't have told you that, should I?" Irene's attitude had suddenly changed, the voice had become a little warmer, her smile suddenly friendlier.

"Exactly what is it that you are—?"

"I want to know where you'll stand—and let you know the only place you can..." Irene paused and then her eyes moved downward. Her face seemed to get slightly red and her hand moved nervously. "No! That's not the truth."

"Oh? The truth?"

There was a strange, wild light in her eyes, calculating, then almost warm, seductive. Her shifting mood was fascinating. The woman was actually rather difficult to read. A very skilled con-artist.

"Not the full truth, anyway," she suggested, almost huskily.

"What isn't?"

"Everything I told you. It was only an excuse to...*to see you!"* The last three words were blurted out. Very convincingly. But he wasn't buying her line. It was too slick. A seductive move; perhaps coldly calculated.

Then her mood changed, altered, as if a switch had been thrown.

Suddenly Irene stood up and started for the door. "I shouldn't have come!"

"Wait!" Haden shouted, a little surprised by the sudden turn. It was the last thing he would have expected. Yet a part of him was intrigued; and, bottom line, very interested in what kind of game she might be playing and what kind of implied or real pleasures it might offer. The woman was, without question, a lovely package any man would just love to bed.

"Please! It was a mistake!"

Irene tried to brush past him, but Haden reached out and took hold of her shoulder, turning her around to face him. For a long time she stared up at him and then, suddenly, without any warning, she impulsively moved close, sliding her arms around his neck and pressing her lips to his.

"Is this what you want? What we want?" she murmured.

The kiss was short but filled with such impact that Haden was left numb. By the time his mental shock and sensual reactions had slipped away, he was alone.

He stood there, staring at the door, stunned and completely confused by what had happened.

He had never thought Irene Kilman had even really noticed him. What had just taken place had no logic or sanity unless he read only one thing into it: she had been secretly and inwardly burning for him;

silently wanting him until she couldn't stand it any longer. So she had come up and.... But it didn't make sense.

But that was foolish egotistic conclusions.

There was something else going on; something illusive, maybe even dangerous. Her swift shift of mood was unnerving.

And he wasn't foolish enough to believe a fantasy about her having secretly desired him for a long time; that was pure crap. It was the one she quite obviously wanted to leave him with. She was a skilled player and he'd be a fool to truly buy into her game.

For a few moments longer he stared at the door, and then took several swallows of his drink. Maybe if he got a little high he would be able to think things out a little more clearly. He had to make sense out of something that was completely insane.

Irene Kilman was known to have her lovers, it wasn't any secret. But this play she'd made was so obvious. And at the same time subtly underscoring a lot of things, including a blocking move to stand between him and her daughter-in-law.

She considered him a serious player. That was interesting and revealing. And her visit was a major blocking move on her part.

The woman was afraid of him!

Amazing reality.

That night Haden dreamed about Irene Kilman.

It was a confusing, vague series of visual images. At one point they were in bed together, only she was still fully dressed, as if this were some kind of secret wall between them. She offered sex, but didn't strip naked before him.

You can have me, honey, but not...

Then suddenly he was awake sitting up in bed, sweat pouring out of every pore in his body, his head throbbing from a slight hangover.

Her last words numbed him: he could have her, but she would never bare herself to him, she would never be naked to his caresses.

The implications of that dream didn't miss him at all.

For hours he lay in bed, restless, unable to sleep again. A sudden desire for Irene had been sparked by her kiss, and Haden knew there was only one road it could lead to. He had to deal with Irene Kilman. And she wasn't about to play fair.

Finally at five-thirty, a half-sleep overcame him till he was jarred alert by the alarm. After a shower and breakfast he was just about to leave the apartment for a morning walk, to try to clear the confusion from. his mind, when the doorbell rang. He answered it to find a man standing there.

A few moments later he was looking at a neatly handwritten message.

Dear Jim,

Last night was a mistake. Please try to forget it happened. The only reason I can give is—for a long time I've noticed you and...well, that isn't really an excuse, but it will have to do. I'm afraid of what might happen if such a situation took place again. Please forgive me. And keep your distance. We don't need that; neither of us. Be smart.

Irene Kilman

Several things stunned him by the note. But one was the surprising fact that she'd sent it. What kind of game was she actually playing? Could it be for real? It didn't make sense; it was almost insane! Or, at least, silly. Foolish. Dangerous. It just didn't make sense. Unless it was one hell of a skillful move by a really hard-lined professional player. After all, she'd walked right into the Kilman family, seduced the old man and become mistress of his home and life. She was the Queen of Kilman Enterprises—just as Gordon was the controlling King of the business end. The two made an interesting power duo; and neither seemed to play into one another's hands.

Yet they were both making moves to keep him off the game board.

What kind of game was really being brought into play?

Suddenly Jim Haden wondered if he was a bit over his head. What was going on he didn't know about or understand? These were very hard-line players who had landed home runs. He was still just up to bat, trying to make his mark in a game already fixed.

CHAPTER SEVEN

As James Haden left the home of Gordon Fuller, it was with difficulty that be managed to keep himself from returning and giving the general manager a large slice of his mind.

Gordon had made it a point to be cold and business-like. He had taken the contract with a mumble and then stated that he wanted to see Haden at the office Monday morning. "There are a few things I want to talk to you about!" No thanks for a job well done. No friendly greetings. Nothing.

Shrugging off the anger, Haden slid behind the wheel of his car and started the engine. There were other matters to be concerned with. The first on the list was Irene Kilman. What had happened the night before was still shaking through his subconscious and conscious minds like a tidal wave gone wild.

And the note this morning. A double wham!

Why had Irene come to see him? Was a passionate urge, or something else. It didn't figure. All of a sudden. Then the note. Was that bait...?

Annoyingly he almost felt out-classed. Whatever he did from this point on had to be done with a lot of smart planning. No more ad-libs; no more impulsive moves; nothing based on over-confidence.

This had to be played out like some major chess

game. And it was for keeps.

A warning bell was ringing over and over again that great danger lay in one false move. Checkmate might be a grave mistake. A graveyard invitation, casket and all, and six feet under ground.

The image startled him. It came surfacing like a hard hammer hitting his consciousness.

Did it have something to do with Bob Kilman's death?

Interestingly enough he didn't seriously consider the young man's end as self-inflicted. Instinct suggested something far darker; something very threatening and dangerous.

Shaking his head, Haden tried to convince himself that this was all foolishness. Imagination. Fantasy.

These were real people; and real people didn't go around killing others without some realistic motive.

Instantly, he realized, that was a bunch of crap. In real life people did horrid things without even thinking twice. In real life anything was possible.

And maybe it was time for him to make his move. Regardless of whatever others were doing, it was obvious they considered him a threat. Well, maybe it was about time he started playing out his immediate hand and see how that effected the chessboard's layout.

He started the car down the road and headed in the direction of the Kilman estate. There was somebody else he wanted to see this afternoon, too. Janet.

And maybe Henry Kilman. What he would say to "Old Man Haden"? He wasn't quite sure, but had the feeling it would be a good idea to talk about

Gordon Fuller and see just where things stood.

If only he could work things out so he didn't have to knife the general manager. That was always a dumb move. Yet he had to position himself so he couldn't be touched by Gordon Fuller.

He *could* quit. And that would place him outside of the man's power. Janet was a lady who could be seduced, regardless. He wasn't fool enough to think her interest in him was anything less than basic school-girl crush that could easily be seduced into a deeply felt love-affair and finally marriage. But without a job in this town would leave him without funds. And it might be difficult to get another real job and position with Gordon Fuller blasting his name around town. It was a small town, and the Kilman's owned it. The only safe action he could take was within the framework of keeping his job. And remaining close to the Kilman's on every possible level.

In this game the winners had to be players on the game board and that was within Kilman Enterprises.

That was one advantage he had was his family connection with the "old man"! That even pre-dated Irene's arrival.

It was his one joker in the stacked deck. His wild card. How that fit in Irene's master chess game he wasn't quite sure.

She was the other joker and nothing to laugh at.

Haden sighed as he pulled the car up to the front of Henry Kilman's house and cut off the engine. For a moment he sat in the car, thinking about Irene and her visit the other night and her little note. This event with Irene had put him in a rather interesting position. Even if shaky. Even if somewhat mysteriously uncertain. Even if in danger!

First, Kilman was a friend of his late father. Second, he was going out with Janet Kilman. Third, Irene, the young, attractive slut who had married Old Man Kilman, was hot for him. Or playing one hell of a skillful counter attack to block his own moves on her daughter-in-law. That put him in a different power position with each member of the Kilman family. But if he started playing all the lines at one time, there was a chance of getting them tangled. Tangled around his neck and then he *would* be out.

Irene Kilman could be a powerful player; and a dangerous threat. She was a woman to have under his control! And that was something to be very careful about. She had to be handled just right. But if Janet or Henry found out about their interplay it would be another serious blunder on both of their parts—and he would be the loser.

Shaking his hand, Haden forced himself to admit the truth. That kiss Irene had given him had sparked something inside his guts. Just how far would she go to checkmate him?

It was a fine tight rope he would be walking if he allowed himself to start on the path toward an affair with Irene. She had all the strings in her hands.

But what a woman! One hell of a seductive, sexy package.

Reluctantly Haden stepped out of the car, not quite sure what he planned to do.

Stepping up to the front door, he rang the bell and waited. The butler finally opened the door and once the man recognized Haden, stepped back to let him in.

"Is Janet in?" Haden asked.

"No, sir, she is out with her father. Only Mrs. Kilman is in, sir."

"Oh, then I had better leave—"

Haden started to turn, about to walk hurriedly out of the house, when Irene Kilman's voice sounded from the living room.

"You certainly *won't* leave!" she cried. "Come on in, Jim!"

Haden hesitated, not wanting to step into the trap that would be there for him. But he had no choice except to tread the tightrope.

Taking a deep breath, he stepped forward, down the hall, hearing the butler close the door behind him. In a few seconds he was standing in the living room, looking across at Irene Kilman.

She was clothed only in a blue and fleecy housecoat. She smiled at him over the rim of a cup of coffee.

"How nice to see you," she said formally, but there was a look in her eyes that seemed to be saying it in a more heatedly pointed way.

"Hello, *Mrs.* Kilman!" he greeted, trying hard to keep his voice as impersonal as possible. He had actually come to see her, in the first place, but now he regretted the action. He realized that, now. All else had been rationalizations. It was a mistake, but now it was too late to do anything about it.

"Sit down, make yourself at home. Have some brunch with me? Some coffee—or something to drink?" she offered, warmly.

"Just some coffee."

Standing, Irene went to a small buzzer and

pressed it. "Now, tell me, what did you come over for?"

She looked down at him, her face serious, but her eyes twinkling. Haden tried to keep his own eyes from her body, which showed voluptuously through the loosely fitting lounging robe.

The top front bulged outward, giving honest testimony of her large breast line. From what little Haden knew about house and lounging robes, women didn't wear any lingerie under them, especially bras. And she was obvious stark naked.

"What did I come over for?" he repeated foolishly, in a dull, flat voice.

"That's what I asked."

Just then the maid came in and Irene Kilman ordered some coffee for him.

In that brief moment Haden had a chance to organize his thoughts. He had to make up his mind exactly how to play this little game, and its slim hand of cards she'd given him. There were several ways—and he didn't like any of them, now that he had the chance to seriously consider them. The women somewhat scared him.

Finally he decided to play it straight, stupid and honest. That might be his only line of attack.

Irene's eyes moved back to him as she seated herself on the sofa, opposite the chair in which he was sitting.

"Well?" she asked, tauntingly.

"Well, if you want to know the truth, I'm a little puzzled."

"About what?" From the tone of her voice she was fully aware of the direction of the conversation, but wanted him to come right out and lay it on the line.

"About your visit last night, and the note."

"I wish you would forget that," she told him, smiling. And again her tone of voice indicated just the opposite.

For a moment Haden didn't say anything. Instead he stared at Irene, revealing open interest in what he saw, while he was trying mentally to decide exactly what the next move going to be.

"Really, Jim, it was a mistake." She didn't even try to make that sound very convincing. Her eyes flirted openly with him, just daring him to make an obvious move.

"Okay. I understand. But why, why at this time?"

"Impulse. Confusion. Depression, I guess. The death of Bob was quite a shock to the whole family. It lingers, ever more, during things last months. To me, too. And I was getting a little…"

"Let's stop the fencing!" Haden suddenly said in a firm voice. "I never liked thrusting and parrying. Best to just hack away! Like you have already done."

For a startled moment Irene stared at him, then slowly a smile moved the corners of her lips upwards. "Okay, let's stop fencing. And hack away. Is that as exciting?"

"Not very. But it cuts through all the crap. So I'm going to be blunt and to the point! Like you were!"

"That might be…interesting."

"You aren't the kind of woman to do things on impulse. You're too ambitious. You have too much at stake. You can't afford to get involved in any complicated relationships that might create some gap between you and your little fortune with Henry Kilman!"

Irene didn't say anything, only looked evenly at Haden, no emotion showing on her pretty features.

"There's a big shakeup coming—I can see it, and I think you know about it." He was shooting in the dark, trying to make statement as general as he could, while at the same time attempting to make it sound like he knew more than he did. A major bluff.

"Your visit last night was a well thought out and planned thing. I'm not the fool you take me for. I'm not an innocent. And what is more, I know a quite a bit about you and your mental attitudes, because they're very much like my own."

"Oh, really. You believe that?" she murmured, almost amused.

"You're a woman who wanted money and social position, and you got it the easy way."

"Meaning, I suppose, screwing myself into his bed? Is that what you're implying?" There wasn't even the hint of annoyance, merely a statement of cold fact. Either that or she was revealing a very skilled control over very real annoyance. Of course she had admitted as much the night before.

He decided to ignore her statement and just continued on as if she had said nothing: "Now what I want to know is why your interest—sudden interest, I might add—is in me!"

For a long time the room was silent, the words were hanging between them like heavy weights. Haden couldn't tell read Irene's reaction to his words, her face had remained blank. The control amazed him. She was more than just a good actress playing out a role. If she'd been a Hollywood star there was no doubt about the fact she'd have received the best acting honors.

"Okay, Mr. Haden," she said finally in clipped words, her tone of voice emotionless. "Since you've been so honest—I'll try to be the same. You're right about a shakeup. What it is, I don't believe I'll tell you. Is that blunt enough for your delicate little ears, young man!"

"Oh, I think you can do better than that," he retorted without reacting to her cutting tone of voice and choice of words.

She merely nodded, pleased, as if enjoying the game that was fashioning itself automatically, without any real effort on her part. "Okay. Just for the fun of it…this much I *will* tell you: we have more than a *little* in common." She paused and then her lips smiled warmly. "So, let's try to be friends? At least act as if we were. Might be a smart play on both our parts. And far more fun. I've always liked you and…well, there's no reason why we can't just act like intelligent adults!"

Just then the maid returned with coffee and handed Haden a cup. Then she left. But the interruption had caused a change of mood. When he turned his eyes back to Irene Kilman, they made direct contact with the top of her house robe, which had opened slightly. By design or by accident, he didn't know. Nor care. It was, now, a part of the game-play, and had to be acted upon. Or openly ignored.

"Do you know when Janet will be back?" Haden asked.

"More or less. Late tonight, if then." There was a twinkle in Irene's green eyes. "Why don't you re-

73

lax, you look...jumpy, as if you wish you weren't here. Do I make you nervous?"

"To be truthful, it *is* a little awkward—after that little event last night."

The silence was heavy and Haden had the uneasy feeling that Irene Kilman was beginning to get the wrong idea of what their relationship should be. Finally she stood and walked across the room. She stopped before a large oak cabinet in which Henry Kilman kept a good healthy liquor supply.

"You'll have a drink with me, won't you?" she asked in a light, airy voice.

"I—"

"Sure you will. I won't take no for an answer!" It only took her a few minutes to mix highballs and then, gliding over to the chair where Haden was sitting, she handed him one of the tall glasses.

"After all, Jim, there's no reason why we can't be friendly. You have to admit that we both have a lot in common. You want Janet for money—I've got Henry already for *that* reason. We think alike—and if you plan on being part of the family, we might as well start getting on good terms."

Haden sipped his drink, nervously. He wanted to get out of the place as fast as possible. There was a look about Irene's eyes and the way the corners of her lovely lips turned upward as she looked into his eyes. The mood had become seductive. The robe seemed open just a slight bit more, revealing soft, full flesh.

"What makes you really think I'm after Janet for money?"

"Let's say that it takes one to know one. You're a con artist. I saw it the moment you came back to

74

town and went to work for Henry. But don't worry, I don't think Janet has the emotional or mental makeup to see through you.

"She's the kind of woman who likes to hear nice things about herself—likes to have a man who loves her. She won't let herself believe anything else. In other words, she is lonely and lost little virgin girl—especially now, since her brother died."

Haden didn't say anything to that, but instead looked gloomily at his highball glass, and then, after a moment of hesitation, he took several large swallows of the liquor. It was hard to keep his eyes away from the beauty and sensual excitement of Irene's figure. She was still standing in front of him, looking down with that half-smile.

"You're nervous about being here!" she observed in an amused voice. "Aren't you?"

"Why?" he countered, defensively. "Why should I be?"

"Because...I think you feel the same way I do about...well...last night!"

"What does that mean?" Haden blurted out, his eyes popping up to meet hers. He saw flaming desire burning down at him, extending from her beautiful eyes.

"I think you know."

"Okay! So you're an attractive woman. I'm a man. And men like attractive women. It's just as simple as that!"

"Is it?" she offered in an openly wondering voice. It was as if she were facing that question for the first time; considering the possibilities and implications.

Haden stared at her for a moment, anger flooding through his mind and body, then suddenly he was standing, reaching for her. He didn't know how it had happened.

It took possession of his body and mind. Then he was aware of the silken, giving texture of Irene's lips against his. They parted and he felt her tongue push past his teeth. Her body was clutching, straining at his, eagerly, hungrily, and desperately. She held nothing back and he could feel the softness of her breasts under the robe.

He felt dizzy with the flood of desire that whipped through every cell and nerve in him.

Then, with a will he hadn't realized he possessed, Haden released Irene, gently pushing her back. For a moment he stared at her and then turned and walked out. He didn't even think until he was in his car and starting the engine. A moment after that he directed the car down the street, in a total mental daze. Shocked at what had happened. Or nearly happened. One moment longer and he would have fairly ripped that rope off her body and totally ravished her.

CHAPTER EIGHT

Connie Gales, Haden thought, disgustedly. She was the only thing that could possibly take the burn from his guts. The burn Irene Kilman had fired. There went his plans to investigate Bob's death. Plans that might have gotten him in a better position with Old Man Kilman.

But it was better than making love to Irene Kilman. That could be the end for him, the end of everything he had been working so hard to get.

Maybe that's the game Irene was playing. Once she'd seduced him it could be used to blackmail him into doing whatever she commanded. On the other hand, couldn't it go the other way, too?

He considered that, then shook his head. Obviously Irene Kilman wasn't at all concerned about her extra marital affairs being discovered by her husband. Surely the old man knew the truth; he wasn't dumb—not at all!

But if he discovered his old friend's son was balling Irene, that might be something totally different. In business the Old Man demanded loyalty above all else.

Haden directed his car toward Connie's apartment. It had been a long week since he had been with Connie. Maybe that was where he should have gone in the first place. Always best to play it safe. Connie was safe.

The trouble with him was that he thought too much. After all, what was it he was attempting to do? Marry Janet Kilman. Get into a rich family and then live the life of ease. To hell with everything else.

Now that was a plan. But for the moment he couldn't make any moves in that direction. So...

Go to Connie's bed. Another lost weekend. Escape.

It took only twenty minutes to arrive at Connie's. Haden parked his car, got out and went into the apartment house.

He knocked on Connie's door.

Waited.

Knocked again.

Waited.

Knocked once more. And waited.

God damn Connie! he thought. *What right did she have to be out when her boss wanted her body?*

None!

Sighing, Haden walked back to his car. He was just beginning to get in when his eyes spotted a small entranceway on his side of the street, with a sign over it!

BAR ENTANCE

He could use a drink. *If you couldn't get a woman there was the other way out. Drink and be merry. If you can't have Mary, then be merry!*

Angrily he slammed his car door and stepped around to the sidewalk. A few moments later he was sipping a Scotch and soda.

It took a little over a half hour before he came to the point where he believed it would be possible to go back home, sleep it off and try to forget everything.

Haden paid his bill and walked out. It was half an hour's drive to his place, because he had to go at a snail's pace in order to keep the car under control.

He was getting out of his car when a voice called him.

"Jim, Jim! *Over here!*"

He turned, trying to focus on where the voice had come from. His mind was slightly numb and fuzzy, and his reactions a little slow.

Irene Kilman was stepping out of a nice, white sports car.

Haden just stood there numb, as she walked forward. She came to a stop a few inches from Haden. She smiled and then extended her hand. "I had just about given you up!"

"What?"

"Take me up to your apartment—we'll talk about it there!"

She took his hand in hers, squeezing gently.

Irene was clothed in a tight-fitting green dress that matched the color of her eyes. The way the cloth fitted her figure and breasts made it all too obvious what she had come to see him for.

"No!" he objected.

"Why?"

"Because...just call it complications!"

"Don't be silly, Jim! Nobody will know."

For a long moment he stared at her, uncertain as to what he should do. Finally he didn't care anymore. The sight of her seduced him.

Why not? he thought, starting to lead her toward the apartment house where he lived. *Why not?*

Haden closed the door behind them and turned and looked at Irene Kilman.

"I hope you know what you're doing," he told her, taking in the full sweep of her body. The high, brimming bust line and the flare of her hips. "I'm certainly not in any condition..."

Irene smiled and moved into his arms. The kiss was warm and probing and long. The effect made him slightly dizzy.

"I know *exactly* what I'm doing," she told him, stepping away and moving across the living room. "You have quite a place here, Jim. Really, I'm surprised! On the money you make from Henry...

"Mr. Kilman pays pretty well."

"I know!" she stated, turning and looking directly at him. "How about a drink?"

"If you want!" Haden pointed toward the small home bar in the corner of the room. "That should help you a little."

"Thanks. Should I help myself—or are..."

"Help yourself. I'll be back in a moment." Haden moved toward the bathroom. He had to think, and this was the only place he knew where it would be possible to be alone.

He didn't like the setup. There was the physical desire, but playing around with the boss' wife was far too dangerous. He'd already decided to avoid Irene's seductive moves. Whatever her game was it didn't offer any safe rewards to him. She was out for Number One: Irene.

Closing the bathroom door and locking it, he

looked at himself in the mirror. He didn't appear drunk. The features that stared back at him were lean and cleanly cut. His eyes looked only a little shiny.

Where was he letting his life go? Here he was, about to be screwed by the wife of an old friend, a man who had been like a father to him in the past years. And what rationalization did he have? Because the woman was a tramp. She'd sleep with anything that wore pants. A sell-out slut!

Bitterly he swallowed hard, and dropped his eyes.

It wasn't easy to look into the features of a bastard, especially when they were his own.

But then, he suddenly realized, wanting to have Janet Kilman marry him for money, wasn't really so noble.

To hell with it all!

Irene was just another bitch in heat and she played by some very wild rules. He was making too much of it. If she wanted to play; then he might as well take her on. They were already past the flirtation stage. This was the real thing. And she had played her cards right out on the table: let's have sex.

Haden turned and moved from the bathroom into the living room.

Irene Kilman was sitting on the sofa, her skirt pulled up over her knees, revealing the beautifully long tapering lines of her legs.

"Well, it took you a long time to do whatever it was you were doing," she announced, smiling and letting her eyes move up and down his body. The expression on her face was the wild look of a woman on the edge of control—an edge she wanted to leap over into whatever pit might exist beyond its limits.

"You sure are one hell of a man, Jim! I don't know why we haven't gotten together before...but then, activities that keep people from circulating in the same circles...well...never mind that. We just missed one another back there...a shame that."

"We were circulating pretty close!" Haden remarked without humor. He walked over to the cabinet and fixed himself a Scotch and soda.

"Not really, not the way I mean!" she explained.

Haden turned and looked at Irene. He took a sip of the Scotch and waited for the effects to burn down his gut.

"Let's not talk about it!" he said.

For a long time they stared at each other, not talking. And the longer he looked at Irene, the greater the feeling that this was all wrong, welled in him. This *should* be Janet—not Irene. It was all wrong!

"I don't like this," Haden finally said in a weak-sounding voice.

"What don't you like about it?" she demanded, eyes narrowing. "Don't you like me?"

"Oh, come on!" he snapped, almost angrily.

She shook her head slightly, brushed aside a lock of hair from her forehead, those eyes continually staring at him, almost wild in their open desire—and something else, less easy to understand. She seemed like a woman possessed by demons.

"Don't you think this is a bit...dangerous, all around?"

"Does that scare you, love?" she murmured,

82

huskily.

"Terrifies me!" he admitted. "To be bluntly frank. You're a confusing puzzle."

"Oh?" she looked amused.

"Yes…one moment seductive, the next all business, and then…suddenly you get very sensually inviting, only to change to a cold-blooded bitch … what kind of game are you playing, Irene?"

It was the first time he'd used her name in such a manner. Almost in a friendly way.

Irene just smiled and then after taking a deep breath, stood and moved over to him. "I don't think that's really important. There are other things going on…between us. You know it, so do I. Emotions grow in a person and they take control, don't you think? And what's about to happen here and now isn't so much emotional as sexual. We're both animals in heat. Adults who play seductive games in the night, or all hours of the day, with whomever might catch our attention. So, let's not play innocent between the two of us. We're two of a kind. So stop quibbling, honey. I'm here to mate with you, love."

She was standing only a few inches from him now, her jutting breasts almost touching his chest. The delicate scent of perfume came intriguingly from her. She looked deep into his eyes, unflinchingly. "It's too late to turn back now! I'm burning all over for you."

Before he knew what had happened, Irene had slid her arms around his neck and pressed her body firmly against his. Her hips were soft and giving. Her breasts were full and supple against his chest. For a long moment she stared into his eyes and then suddenly their lips were touching. Her mouth was warm and moist and open, eager, and he felt the anxious, almost savagely hungry probe of her tongue as it moved into between his lips.

Helplessly, Haden folded his arms around her lush body, unable to control the lusts and desires any longer. The mental resistance was overwhelmed by the bodily ache.

There was no turning back now, as she had said. Her legs pressed against his thighs

"Let's...stop playing...games," she moaned in his ear, as her lips caressingly pressed its lobe between their inner silken surfaces.

Like a man held in the grip of a strong vice, Haden felt himself being led into the bedroom. Irene closed the door behind them.

Without waiting for him, she started to remove her dress. It slid down in a circle around her legs, and she daintily stepped out of it, while beginning to work with the clasp of her bra. A moment after that she was slipping out of her panties.

"What you waiting for?" she asked, staring half amused at Haden. "Come on! Let me see that hard body of yours!"

It was only a matter of a few seconds for Haden to undress and then they slid down to the bed, clutching savagely at each other.

It was like being in a nightmare in which you struggle mentally to escape, but are physically unable. Her body moved against his, squirming slightly, her hands leading his over the mounds of her breasts and down to her stomach and then lower, until she was moaning and whipping under him.

Her whole body moved convulsively as his lips slid down to her breasts, exploring the supple, silky skin, and then working the rigid nipples. Her hands clawed at the back of his head, pushing him deeper into the roundness of her giving breasts.

Finally her head thrashed violently and a sob sounded from her lips.

"Don't wait…" she cried in desperate excitement, shifting her legs and pulling him tighter to her, straining hungrily until they joined and began the sensual rhythms of an erotic dance that sent waves of pleasure between them. An amazing electric ecstasy rippled through them, leaving each exhausted and satisfied for the moment.

Haden knew it was only a matter of a short time before she'd be at him again. The woman proved even more amazing than he expect. Suddenly she was once again in his arms, smoothing him with hot, hungry kisses that ran down his body with such a fury that all he could do was lay there, bathing in the wonderful sensation her loving lips created. She feasted on him as if she could never get enough, then suddenly they were on united force, driving at one another like savage beasts, devouring sensation after sensation as they ravished one another time and again.

SEX IS MY BUSINESS, BY CHARLES NUETZEL

CHAPTER NINE

It was with a dry, defeated feeling that James Haden awoke the next morning. His first thought was about Irene and he turned in the bed to look at her.

She wasn't there.

Cold sweat covered his body as his eyes searched the room for her or her clothing. There was no sign of the woman, or that she had even been there.

For a moment he had the vague idea it had all been a dream; that Irene Kilman hadn't been waiting for him outside his apartment. That she hadn't come up here with him.

But he knew that wasn't true. She had been amazing, driving him beyond normal limits.

Sighing, Haden slipped out of bed and half stumbled out of the room. It took him only a few seconds to spot a small white envelope on the kitchen table, with his name written on it.

Hurriedly Haden tore the envelope open and read the short message.

Dear Jim,

I felt it better that I leave in the

night, so that I'd be home at a proper hour. I guess you understand.

Irene

Both relief and fear knotted in his gut, twisting through his whole body. What was going to happen now? If Henry ever found out, it would be the end of every effort Jim had taken to get into the Kilman family. It Janet learned what had happened, it would *really* be the end for him! It was one thing to carry on an affair with a secretary, but quite another thing to sleep with a stepmother.

But there wasn't anything he could do about it now. It was too late. The best chance he had was to see that it never happened again.

But now he knew what it felt like to be overwhelmed by Irene Kilman. Yet he couldn't let them be together ever again.

He had to stop; cold!

And that was exactly what he expected to happen.

* * * * * * *

Janet Kilman sat out by the pool, looking toward the house. It seemed to her that so many things had changed since her father had married Irene. It was almost as if the house weren't home any more. None of the love or tenderness or warmth she had felt in the past had any place in the present.

Her father was wholly taken in by the little slut he had married, playing with his new toy, and never really noticing the outside world, or those closest to him. The death of Bob had jarred her father, but then, he had gone back to his escape.

Janet moved a lock of golden hair from her forehead. Last night she had been awakened by a creeping sound outside her room, in the hallway. The light tip-tapping, hardly above a whisper, had told her it was Irene returning home.

Janet wasn't the fool her father had become. She knew Irene Kilman had been having a little fun on the side. But that was her father's business and she wasn't about to get into it.

Remain silent. And think about something else. That was the best method.

Idly, Janet looked down at the pool, watching the reflection of the sun dance wildly on its shiny surface. It was some time before James Haden drifted into her thoughts. But he finally came, as he had been coming so many times to her thoughts in the past weeks. There was something about the man that made Janet feel both tender and a little afraid. Actually somewhat terrified.

The trouble with her was the she still hadn't really matured emotionally. There were reasons for that.

Janet's mother had been a very prudish woman, with rigid moral ideals that had become outdated even in her own generation.

With such conditioning, even against the reality of the world surrounding her, Janet found it almost impossible to break through the mental resistance. Her body wanted the feel of a man against it, but her mind was rigidly fearful.

"Miss Janet," the voice of Milly, their household maid, called from the porch a few yards behind the pool.

Janet looked up. "Yes?"

"There's a call for you."

"I'll take it in the den."

Janet got up, walked across the patio and into the house. A few moments later she was in the den, the doors closed. Picking up the receiver she said: "Hello?"

"Janet, this is Jim Haden."

"Oh, hello, how are you?" She tried to hide the excitement in her voice. It had been a long while since she'd heard from him, and now suddenly she realized how much she *really* had wanted to hear from Haden.

"It was wondering if you're doing anything this afternoon."

"Nothing much, nothing much at all, Jim."

"Like to go for a ride, dinner, dancing—the whole works?"

She didn't need to think about that for long. "Yes!"

They talked for a few moments longer and he told her he would be there in about an hour. Then she hung up. Her face was smiling and her heart beginning to pound. That was surprising to Janet, because she hadn't realized how much she was drawn to Haden. The conversation was a blur and the only thing she remembered about it that she had less than sixty minutes to get ready for a date with this wonderfully exciting male.

At that very moment she almost felt as if he could have seduced her royally without so much as a gasp of voluptuous excitement from her.

On second thought, Janet strictly instructed herself, no seductive games!

No games? She wondered. Yet she planned on dressing to kill! She wanted him to want her so bad that he couldn't keep his eyes or hands off her.

As she was walking from the room Janet suddenly stopped, stunned. All at once her mind had pin-pointed the reason for her excitement—beyond the fact of seeing Haden.

If the chance came, she was going to let him make love to her.

That thought shocked Janet. *What in the world had made her think it? What mental action had caused her to come to that conclusion?*

Yet she feared this was the basic truth, the real reason for her flush of total excitement at being out with Haden.

Shaking slightly, Janet walked down the hall toward the stairs which led up to her room. Like a zombie, she moved up the stairs, numb in the knowledge that regardless of everything else, she *really* was planning on getting herself seduced!

Or at the very least, teasing herself with that fantasy.

Could she really go through with such a thing? Haden, quite obviously, would willingly take her anywhere she wanted to go. That much she realized.

Janet might be inexperienced sexually but not a fool. She was smart enough to size a man up and knew pretty much what this one wanted. Why didn't even bother her.

James Haden wanted to seduce her. That was obvious. And suddenly she realized how much she wanted to be with him in every possible way; intimately involved with this delightfully lovely male animal.

She had been in love with him for a very long time.

This was a chance to break away from the old life pattern she realized. But why? Why so suddenly? That was what puzzled her.

All her life she'd lived in a world of strict moral ethics. And now, at twenty-five she suddenly realized that it was about to shatter around her, because this was what she *wanted!*

Anyway, she reasoned, *what had she been really saving it for? What purpose, when practically everyone her age and even younger didn't? Very few virgins left in the world.*

Maybe, after tonight, there would be on less virgin.

She was somewhat shocked by this realization. And that was very frightening.

CHAPTER TEN

All the way over to the Kilman home, Haden kept wondering what insanity had crazed him to call Janet for a date, the very morning after having slept with Irene Kilman. It didn't make sense even to him, sane or not.

Yet there had been an inner drive to be with Janet.

Maybe it was caused by the desire to show Irene Kilman that what had happened didn't change things.

That he was ignoring their little session together.

Finally he arrived at the house and was thankful that he didn't accidentally meet either Henry or Irene. Janet was waiting for him and came to the door when he rang.

"Well, ready, already?" he asked, a little surprised to see her standing there.

She had on a white, starched dress with a low neckline. White gloves were on her hands. She smiled up brightly at him, and he detected a slight flush to her cheeks.

Janet was a very pretty woman. Young and innocent. What he planned for her was a dirty trick. But people have to grab what they can. Janet Kilman meant an easy life for him and he was determined to have it. And anyway he would be giving her a good life. He knew how to make women enjoy sex, and that would be one thing that he could give their marriage.

It was odd, how he simply accepted the fact that Janet would take him as her husband. And that was because he also knew his women. Once he had convinced her that she needed him, the rest would be easy.

"Well, what do you want to do?" Haden asked as they seated themselves in his car.

"I couldn't care less," Janet answered brightly. Leaning closer to him, she placed a delicate hand on his arm. "Anything you want to do."

If it had been anybody except Janet Kilman, Jim would have considered that an open invitation to take her to a motel, immediately!

"Okay, how about a ride out in the country. I know a nice club outside of town. *The Hanging Tree.*"

"That would be wonderful!" Janet exclaimed excitedly. "I've been there once. A lovely place. And we can dance and do a…" Her voice faded out, and she looked at him nervously. After a moment her eyes dropped.

He waited a few seconds and then started the engine.

It took them a little over an hour to get to *The Hanging Tree*. They sat in the cocktail lounge, sipping martinis and talking. The conversation was fairly light and general until suddenly Janet turned it to more serious subjects.

"How does a man feel about a woman who has

let him make love to her?" The question came so unexpected that he was taken aback. It was out of context to the conversation. One moment it had been generalities—and then suddenly Janet had blurted out this question.

"What the hell made me say that?" she asked before he could answer the question. Her face was flushed red and her eyes seemed to have difficulty finding a spot on which to focus.

Haden knew all too well what she was leading up to, and what had made her say that. And he was shocked realization that he couldn't take advantage of her!

"Let's not worry about that," he said carefully, avoiding her eyes.

There was a heavy silence after that, and then finally Janet said in an even, determined voice: "On second thought I believe I *would* like to continue *that* conversation!"

Haden looked up at her and was surprised to see the open desire in her eyes. But there was another emotion, revealed in the red tint of her face. Embarrassment.

"Look, Janet, you're a nice girl. Don't make the mistake of...well, getting involved in *that* way."

For a moment she hesitated, then asked: "What makes you really think I'm such a nice girl? There's no reason for you to think that. After all, what do you *really* know about me?

"I mean, well, you've never actually made a blunt, forward pass. It's been only...after all, I'm not a child, and there's no reason to treat me like one!"

The anger of her words was directed more toward herself than Haden; it was so obvious that he

95

found it hard to keep from smiling.

"Look, Janet. I...well, I just know you aren't the kind of woman to take lightly—to...well, to be blunt: you're the marrying kind! Not a free swinging woman."

Haden was surprised by his own words. This was what he had been trying to build up to, and now he was going out of his way to stop it before it got started. An affair would make it easy to take the next, more permanent step.

"Look, Janet—don't make the mistake...it's all too tempting. You're a beautiful woman—and to be honest, it wouldn't be hard to make love to you—in fact I can't think of anything that I want to do more! Making love to you. And that's what it would be. Love—or not at all!"

"Oh, shut up!" she snapped, angrily. "This is ridiculous, and I want to forget the subject came up!"

The dinner was a stilted and cold affair after that, and Haden realized the evening was shot to hell and back. The damage was done and there wasn't anything that could be done about it now. Maybe later in the evening, but not now.

When they were through he offered to order drinks, but Janet declined. "I think it might be better if you just took me home!"

And that was that. He paid the bill and a little later they were out in the car, driving back toward the Kilman home.

Haden couldn't help feeling a sense of depression. It had been laid out there for him to pick up, and yet something within him had been repelled.

It wasn't just the fact that he had rejected a night

with Janet that bothered him, but rather the mental resistance that had caused him to refuse her offer. He had, in effect, turned of down.

They didn't talk all the way back to the Kilman home, and when he brought the car to a stop, Janet started to get out.

"Wait, Jan!" he urged, reaching out and taking hold of her shoulder. "Please!"

It was a couple of seconds before she slowly turned and faced him. "What is it you want?"

"Look, I don't like...well, this is not the...damn it all, *I love you!"*

That blurted out so impulsively, without any consideration of the implications that he could hardly believe it.

There was a flicker of surprise and confusion in her eyes. She didn't say anything, just sat waiting for him to continue.

Haden felt like a bastard, but it was a serious, real-life game he was playing, and the stakes were worth the lies. If that was what they were. Even he couldn't be certain.

"Look, Jan, there's not a woman in the world that I care for in the way I care for you—there never has been. I've been fighting it, but...well, there's just no way of fighting emotions. What I mean to say is that...well, damn it all, won't we be seeing each other again?"

Janet continued to stare at him for a long while, and then finally said, "I don't know. It's all happening a little fast. Let me think about it."

Haden urged her toward him, and much to his surprise she moved eagerly and willingly into his arms. The feel of her body was delicious and wonderful. Silky and supple.

Her lips made contact with his and clung for a long time, open and moist. The kiss exploded through Haden like electric fire.

Never before had he felt such an explosive reaction!

There had been many women before in his past, but none that could create such a response in him.

Not even Irene had had that much impact on him. And she was simply great.

He was still trying to recover when he felt Janet slip away from his arms and move across the seat and open the door.

"Call me tomorrow, if you...want to," she said in a shaking, frightened voice.

Haden started to stop her, but then decided against it. He was too stunned physically to really move from the car at that moment—and it might not he such a bad idea to play it close to the chest.

"I'll go up by myself," she told him, stepping out of the car and walking across the large yard, up to the huge entranceway. After a moment of fumbling in her purse, she got her key, and a second later she slipped into the house, closing the door behind her.

CHAPTER ELEVEN

Inner frustration had caused Connie Gales to pick up the man from the cheap bar. It was a combination of need for sexual release and the emotional stress caused by her blowup with Dale Robbins.

Nothing she could do had made Dale realize that she really liked him and wanted him. The thing was, she realized, his pride had been hurt; and that was one thing a man like Dale wasn't able to take lightly.

She felt, through the drunken haze, the eager lips of the brute on top of her.

The strange man was a crud, taking what was offered without any interest in whether the woman was enjoying herself.

She was hardly aware of what was happening, and didn't really care. Her mind was in numbed by the booze and her thoughts about Dale Robbins. She didn't care about anything, but getting it over with this pickup.

Then they shifted to images of her boss: Haden.

She lay there, letting him finish, and then he moved away in the darkness.

A moment later he walked from the room, across the living room and then out of the apartment.

He had gotten what he came for, and like the brute he was, had left.

But he had also left behind him a completely confused and emotionally frightened woman. For the first time in her life the idea of being used by a man was disgusting.

She didn't want that kind of life. She wanted something more lasting, something more meaningful, something with Jim Haden.

The instant she thought that Connie realized it was wrong. Haden was a user, too; a more sophisticated one than a pickup at some bar—but just the same animal.

Instead of dreaming about him in her drunken mental fog, she was crying, deep raking sobs. It was a long time before consciousness slipped. Nightmares came about men taking her into strange dark rooms; and they always ended up with Jim Haden's face.

* * * * * * *

Janet Kilman lay on her bed, thinking about what had taken place in the car with James Haden. She couldn't help feeling a certain amount of mental confusion. His sudden statement that he loved her ha left Janet a little numb. She didn't know exactly how to react to the statement—she didn't know how she even *felt* about it.

At dinner she had done everything possible to lead the conversation toward sex. But now she realized what a crude and awkward job she had done. And in embarrassed frustration that she'd made a complete mess of the job.

100

After all, he had been a friend of the family for long time. And it *would,* possibly, be awkward, having an affair with her. It was just too close a relationship

Yet, it all seemed strange to Janet. She was sure he was having an affair with his secretary, Connie Gales.

Janet moved nervously in bed, wanting sleep to come.

Oh, God how she wanted to...be done with all this virginity business. To be made a complete woman!

And how could that happen until she stopped being a foolish little child?

What could a girl like her do? Go out and pick up somebody on the street?

No, no way.

She wasn't a cheap little slut.

But...

A love affair with a man you cared about was something else. Even if it didn't end in marriage.

At least a romance with somebody she loved...

Abruptly stopped her thoughts, cold. For a long time she tried to block all mental activity. Then, slowly, the truth kept floating to the surface: *she* was *in love with Haden, otherwise she would never have been willing to have an affair with him.*

Janet found herself startled, even frightened, by the realization, but at the same time less conflicted.

Her whole body began slowly to float on a sea of restfulness, and then the conscious world started to fade away, until she was conscious only of dreaming.

CHAPTER TWELVE

James Haden looked at the general manager and felt a nervous grind circle through his guts. There was an inner feeling of hate and anger at the man's attitude.

"These contracts are not too good!" Gordon stated nastily. "You might have done better.

"You know damned well they're good!" James Haden cried back, feeling the tension grip through his body once more. "They were the best I could get."

"Then maybe we could have another person do the job, next time!" Gordon leaned forward and stared heatedly at Haden.

"Like I told you the other day—there'll be no more sliding along on your belly! You'll have to work—and work hard. You can go now!'

Haden stared at the other man, surprised. He had been called into the general manager's office to only be told that the contracts he had signed with the government weren't good enough.

Gordon knew damned well they were plenty good enough. With the government you had to be careful, and all you could do was hope for the best.

Slowly he stood up and started out of the office.

It would be only a matter of weeks before

Gordon Fuller found reason to fire him, and that would make things awkward for both Haden and Old Man Kilman But, if he became engaged to Janet Kilman then Gordon couldn't touch him.

Haden decided the only thing was to arrange a date in the mountains or on the beach, for the weekend. Janet wanted an affair, that much she had indicated fairly obviously the other night. Once an affair started, it wouldn't be hard to rush her right into marriage.

When Haden reached his office he had Connie call the Kilman home. A moment later he said:

"Hello, Jan, how are things?"

"Oh Jim, I'm so glad to hear from you! After what you said last night...I was a little confused and didn't really act very nice."

"Forget it." Haden paused and then said in a hesitant voice. "I was wondering, Jan, would you like to go up to the mountains with me this weekend?"

There was a long silence and then Janet suddenly blurted out: "Why not?"

* * * * * * *

Henry Kilman stepped into the General Manager's office and nodded grimly.

"How're you, Gordon?" he asked, moving into the chair opposite the man.

"Fine, sir. The only thing is...I don't know quite how to tell you this, since he's such a good friend of your family—actually I'm glad you came in."

"What are you gibbering about?" the older man demanded, irritation shading his voice.

104

"It's about James Haden."

"Well, what about him?"

"I just don't see how he's going to work out!"

Kilman stared at the other man for a long time in silence, his face a hard stone, expressionless and cold. Finally he leaned forward and said: "Gordon, I don't care much if he is a terrible worker. I owe him a lot—and that's the beginning and the end of it!"

Gordon Fuller's face blanched and his eyes widened in surprise. "I don't get it?"

"Well Jim doesn't know it, but his father saved my life years ago, when we were boys, and I never had a chance to repay the debt. When his father died I promised him I'd look after Jim. That's what I'm doing."

Kilman paused and then asked, "Now just what is it you think Jim has been doing?"

"Well, these government contracts, I don't believe they show the best effort on his part."

"I don't see what was wrong with them"

Cordon Fuller started to say something but Kilman cut him short with a jerk of his hand.

"I'll have a talk with Jim—and we'll see what happens. In the meantime you take care of everything here. I don't want to be bothered with details."

Henry Kilman stood up and then walked out of the office.

* * * * * *

It was about four in the afternoon when Connie Gales came into Haden's office and said: "Mr. Kilman called and asked you over for dinner at his place. Can you accept?"

"Of course. Even if I couldn't, I would. You don't say no to the boss!"

It took Haden several minutes to think over the invitation and realize there was something odd about it. Usually when Henry Kilman wanted him over, it was done in a more or less informal way. Shaking his head, he forced the thoughts from his mind and returned his attention to the business at hand.

When the day was finished he went home, showered, changed his clothes and then drove to the Kilman estate.

The butler let him in and directed him to go to Kilman's private study.

"What's up?

"Don't know, sir," the man answered.

Puzzled, Haden moved down the long hall, not even conscious of the huge oil paintings that lined the walls. He had been there too many times to he aware of the details of his surroundings. The wall-to-wall lush carpeting, the heavy oak furnishings and paintings all blended into a single impact: Kilman Estate.

Haden opened the door of the study and looked in.

"Henry?" he said softly.

"Oh, come on in!" the gruff voice called from out of sight of the door.

Haden stepped into the room, closing the door behind him. This was the one place in the house that held the greatest interest for Haden, with its bookcase walls filled with all the knowledge of man from all time. In the middle of the room was a dark oak desk with a leather swivel chair.

106

Henry Kilman stepped forward and took Haden's hand firmly in his. "Haven't seen you for some days now. How are things going at the office?"

"Fine, I guess." Haden smiled.

"Come on over here, I want to talk to you a little bit about the...office."

Suddenly Haden began to get the whole message. Somehow Gordon Fuller put a few dirty words in the old man's ear. Jim followed Kilman over to the oak desk and sat in the small chair opposite the huge one behind the desk into which Henry Kilman surged.

For a few seconds Kilman sat, his beefy hands folded on top of the desk, his eyes examining the fingers in minute detail. Finally he shifted his gaze into Haden's eyes. "Jim, Gordon had a few things to say about you this morning."

Haden just nodded.

"I've known you a long time, boy, and I don't think you could lie to me without me guessing it. Your eyes give you away. I guess that's because you're like a second son...well, like a son to me."

"Thank you, sir."

"What I want to know is if you think those contracts were any good—if you think you got the best deal possible."

"I did. That's all that I can say. I pushed and worked hard. Gordon is after my skin!"

Henry Kilman chuckled and then said: "And I can well understand that. He's after Janet. I'd rather have *you* win. But that's up to my daughter—that is, considering that she could fall in love with either of you."

"I told Janet how I felt about her the other evening."

"And what was that?" Henry Kilman asked, interest lighting his face.

"That I love her." Haden felt like kicking himself all over the room and then up the ceiling and across to the other side and down to the floor again.

"How'd she take it?"

"We thought we'd go up to the mountains this weekend." Haden knew there was only one way to play this part of the game. Directly.

A frown creased Henry Kilman's forehead and his eyes narrowed. For a moment his lips moved and then froze.

After a couple of seconds he relaxed and said, "I guess it's none of my business. And anyway I know you well enough to realize you wouldn't take advantage of such a situation with Janet! And if you did—I guess Jan is old enough to know what she's doing."

There was a heaviness to Kilman's voice, and his eyes seemed sad. Suddenly he blurted out: "I just hope you're not planning…"

"That's really not part of the plans. Just a weekend. Your daughter is very attractive. But we're adults, and between intelligent adults there just isn't such a thing as a sordid seduction. If that's what you mean. You should know me better than that! I'm in love with Janet and I hope she's in love with me—I certainly wouldn't do anything to hurt that—let alone to hurt my relationship with you. That's the reason I mentioned it to you, so that you'd understand the truth."

"I'm glad you did, Jim. Only a gentleman would

have come right out and state he was putting my daughter...well, anyway—Janet is old enough to do what she wants! Christ, I don't like the drift of this conversation, to be truthful."

The man looked awkwardly at the far wall, then returned his gaze to the younger man. "Silly, all this. But a father is a father. And regardless we never outgrow our concern over children. And she's a dear. And I would be very pushed out if you were...well, we know your reputation! Oh, don't try to lie to me. I know just about every woman you've been with—how often and...well, you are the typical single man...how do they say it, on the make!"

"Please," Haden quickly said. "That has nothing to do with Jan."

"I would hope not. And I'd hope you clean up your act in that department if you plan on anything serious with her. I can be very nasty if crossed!"

There was a long silence, then the man laughed, a bit loudly. "Come on, kid. I know what it was like to be young and...well, even in middle age I enjoyed it all. Power, man, it is all power. And with power comes the need to use it. Don't forget that. Power is a very strong drug. And men in my position use it with anybody and for any thing. And women are drawn to that power like a moth to fire. Just do me a favor and don't abuse my friendship to you by making a mess of things with Janet. You understand what I mean. I'm certain. You're a fine lad, regardless of all that other stuff. And I hope she plays you fair, too. She's not a fool. She's young. Yes. But hardly a fool."

The man stood, to finalize things, and added: "I know the game. I know the dangers. I know what

Gordon wants and I know what you want. More than you realize, son. But you must, also, know the rules: you're out there on your own and you best not screw things up—and I mean that on a lot of levels. Business is one thing. This…with Jan had best be something else."

"I told you, sir, I'm in love with her!" he announced, hoping it sounded convincing. The very idea was scary; he had not really been serious for a woman for years. Janet was a woman a beautiful young woman. And he was deeply attracted to her; and they'd been friends for a long time. And friendship was an important thing to have before love even entered into a relationship.

And the whole thing was somewhat confused in his mind. But, at the same time, he felt a sense of relief.

Maybe he did love Jan. In some way. At least that was a smart solution to everything.

"Well, now, let's go out and join the rest of the family!" Kilman announced, standing and moving around the desk. "There's dinner—roast chicken!"

CHAPTER THIRTEEN

The drive up to the mountains was filled with inner depression for James Haden. His conversation was light and gay and Janet's responses were light enough, but there was the hammering aching in guts that kept making him hate what was going to happen that weekend.

Guilt didn't become him.

It was like selling himself out. After all Henry Kilman had done for him in the past, now he was using the man's daughter to get himself higher on the social ladder. It was one thing to work hard at a job and fight your way up.

But Janet was innocent and nice; gaily happy at the adventure about to take place. He knew she hadn't had much experience with men. It would be like taking money from a blind person.

And Janet was being fooled about his feelings for her. Janet believed he was in love with her.

"How much farther?" Janet asked, breaking into his thoughts.

"About an hour or so—want to stop off some place to eat? Cocktails?"

"Sure, why not?" she answered, her voice light and happy sounding. She was like a young, daring kid, having an adventure.

It was another five minutes before they spotted a restaurant interesting enough to stop at. It was a large place that featured steaks and cocktails.

Haden pulled the car into the parking lot and cut off the engine. "Well, here we are," he announced, stepping from the car and then around it, opening the door on Janet's side and helping her out.

Her hand was soft and giving in his, and Haden couldn't help feeling a sense of excitement at the contact. If he could say nothing for Janet beside the fact that she attractive at hell, that would be enough. But there was a strong physical spark between them.

Even as kids they had gotten along pretty well, and there had been one heavy petting session when they were in high school. But it hadn't developed beyond that, because both of them were too afraid. And teenagers and she was younger.

Since he'd returned to town, and had started dating Janet, she was experienced enough in dating to know how to keep him at a safe distance. It had been a slow process to get her to this point. And now Haden felt like a bastard. Why he couldn't understand. Not really.

They walked into the cocktail lounge and settled in a dark booth. The cocktail waitress came up and took their orders. A few moments later the two martinis were served, and Haden picked up his cocktail and saluted Janet. "To a wonderful weekend."

Janet looked nervously down at the martini and then the corners of her lips hesitantly moved upward into a forced smile.

"You sure you want to go through with this?"

Not a smart line, he thought, annoyed by his words.

112

Janet nodded and took a sip of her drink.

"What's bothering you, Jim?" she asked after a second, her eyes moving up to gaze into his. "You act like you wish you hadn't asked me to come with you."

Haden thought that over for a few seconds, trying to figure out exactly how he did feel. There really wasn't any reason for him to be so stupid about the whole affair. Janet was a grown woman and she knew what she was getting into. Even her father was reluctantly accepting that fact.

"Forget I asked it," he told Janet, taking a large swallow of his drink. "Let's forget the serious side of the matter—and have fun. That's what we're out for, and nothing else. I don't know what's wrong with me. Maybe just nerves."

Janet smiled and then said: "You act like I was a kid of something."

"Forget it!" Haden snapped angrily.

Janet frowned and then turned her eyes back to the martini glass. There was an awkward silence after that, and for a long time neither of them really relaxed. Haden ordered another round of drinks and then after they had finished them, they went into the dining room and ordered dinner

The conversation didn't pick up until they had a third martini and even then it was purely a surface gaiety. Each was concerned with their own inner thoughts. Finally the dinner was finished and Haden was glad to pay the bill and get out of the place, hoping that in the car they could break the heavy mood.

It was another hour's drive to the mountain resort, and it was driven in almost complete silence.

When they arrived at *Bennings Inn,* the place where Haden had made reservations, Janet was sleeping, with her head resting on the door and seat.

"Janet," Haden said, shaking her shoulder slightly.

Janet slowly moved and then her eyes opened.

"Here already?" she asked, smiling nervously.

"All here!"

They got out of the car, getting their luggage from the trunk, and then walked into the Inn. Haden stepped up to the night clerk and said, "There are rooms for Mr. Haden and Miss Kilman."

The clerk looked up and nodded. "Yes, you called the other day. I have the rooms all ready. Been expecting you. Numbers 203 and 205. They're right next to each other."

"Thanks."

"Just sign there...I'll get the bellboy and have him take you up there."

"Could you have some drinks sent up?"

"Certainly. To...to which room?"

"Mine."

"I guess you'll be taking 208, then?"

"Fine."

The walk to their rooms seemed an endless torment to Haden. It was like walking to a destination that had been mapped out for him by some evil, depraved destiny over which he had no control.

The bellboy opened the door to Room 205 first and took in Janet's luggage.

"I'll be only a few minutes," she told Jim in a low whisper, brushing her lips to his ear. The contact was so sensual that Haden had a rushing sensation of excitement; but it only lasted for a moment.

Haden nodded and then turned toward 203 and waited for the bellboy to open the door. After tipping the man he said: "You'll bring the drinks right away? And ice and soda. A lot of soda."

Haden closed the door behind him and looked at the modern room, feeling like a degenerate.

Hell, what was wrong with him? he cursed inwardly. This was what he had been working for. Janet was just another woman and he had his share of them—both experienced and virgin. *So what the hell?*

With somebody like Connie he'd be ravishing her all ready. And without any sense of guilt.

Going over to the bed and opening his luggage, he started taking his suit and shirts and pants out and hanging them in the closet. Finally he shoved the luggage under the bed and sat down on it.

For a long time he sat waited, thinking. Finally there was a knock on the door. His guts tightened and it seemed his heart gripped. Suddenly he was sweating.

"Just a second," he called out.

"The drinks, sir," came a male voice.

Haden let out a deep sigh of relief. Standing up, he moved to the door, opened it and then waited as the bellboy walked in. After paying for the bottle and the mix and tipping the man, he closed the door.

For a moment he stood looking at the bottle, and then walked over to the desk where it stood. Opening it, he poured a strong triple shot and started gulping it. The more he drank, the better he felt. The hot fire burned down his throat and into his stomach, heating and then numbing it. A few more gulps and his head felt that tight, soothing band around it.

Just another broad about to discover the thrill of James Haden, lover!

Nothing more.

And that was a lie he wanted to believe.

He felt better. Maybe he was just a fool. Janet knew what they had come to the mountains to enjoy. A romantic interlude. With the man who claimed to love her.

What was keeping Janet, anyway? She should have been her before now, he thought, nervously, lighting a cigarette.

There was a knock on the door.

"Yes?"

"Janet," came a quiet, almost hesitant voice. "Who else did you expect?"

For a moment Haden stood there looking at the door, almost afraid to move to it. Then, taking a deep breath he stepped forward and swung the door open.

He felt like the virgin about to be seduced. He felt trapped. There was no escape. Not now.

For a frozen second, Haden stared at Janet before motioning her in. She had put on a low-cut black dress that clung tightly against her stunning young figure.

"Come on in, beautiful," he offered, stepping hack and waiting for her to enter. He closed the door behind her and then leaned back against it, staring at Janet.

"You *are* really something!" he told her. His voice was strangely husky.

"You like me?" she breathed, happily, turning and letting him get a full view of her figure. The back of the dress had a long zipper running from top

116

to bottom of her back.

"How about a drink?" she asked.

"Why not?"

Haden was glad to have something to do besides just standing and staring at Janet. Walking over to the desk, he poured her a drink and put a little soda in it.

"Here's one that will relax you," he announced, handing the drink to Janet.

"Thanks," she whispered, making her lips pout.

Suddenly he wondered what had made him feel this was all wrong. Janet was made for love.

"What's wrong? Janet asked, staring at him wit a puzzled expression working her pouting lips.

"Nothing—nothing at all!" Haden exclaimed, suddenly uneasy. "Just than you're about the most beautiful female I've ever seen!"

Janet laughed nervously, "And what about Connie Gales?"

Haden managed to keep the surprise from his face. "What are you talking about?"

"Oh, I'm not the fool you might think." Jane hesitated for a moment and then continued, smiling "Don't look so shocked!"

Janet broke off, abruptly, flustered. "Let's not tall about such things."

Janet moved toward him, and before he could do anything about it, she had slid her arms around his neck and pressed her body firmly against his.

She felt delicious. Giving and warm. Pulsing with life and passion. Her lips parted and her eyes half closed as she moved her mouth up to his.

"I want you to make love to me, Jim. More than anything in the world."

SEX IS MY BUSINESS, BY CHARLES NUETZEL

CHAPTER FOURTEEN

It took Janet only a few movements to take off the black dress. Much to Haden's surprise there wasn't anything on underneath. She stood before him, smiling brightly, completely naked. For a long time Haden stared, taking in the loveliness of her.

Janet's figure was surprisingly firm and full for a girl her size. Her breasts stood up rigidly, the nipples centered perfectly, pointed and waiting. Her hips, rounded and creamy. Her whole body had perfect, creamy skin, flawless in its silk-like texture.

"What's with you?" she giggled, shocking Haden by reaching out two delicate hands and starting to *work* the buckle of his pants. Before he could do anything to help or stop her, Janet had dropped his pants to the floor around his feet.

"Hurry!" she cried excitedly.

Haden helped her, and in moments he was as naked as Janet. The two of them stared at each other and then suddenly each reached out for the other and they were abruptly clawing heatedly at one another, their nakedness pressing anxiously together.

The kiss was long and moist. There was no turning back; this was the moment he knew had to happen one way or another. And she had made it so easy for him. Haden pulled her up into his arms and

119

then turned and laid her down on the bed, sliding next to her.

For a long while they only held one another, breathing hard, fully aware of the physical contact and the responses which were whipping through their twined bodies. It started slowly, beginning with the urge, desire, longing. Then it developed into gentle muscular movements, and after a few seconds, light caresses.

All at once their bodies were straining against one another, their mouths hungrily devouring, anxiously caressing.

Haden felt himself being urged downward, toward and then Janet's hands pressed his hand forcefully against her breasts, as his lips kissed, caressed.

She might be a virgin, but she was hardly meek or passive.

The delicious excitement of her body squirming and thrusting, jerking and convulsively trembling under his, finally built the peak of desire beyond the point of control—and then Haden felt himself explode, as ecstasy raced through his body like a torrent of over-whelming pain and pleasure, tensing him like rigid steel and then finally relaxing him to a state of exhaustion.

It was a long time before Haden moved or could even think. And when thoughts finally began surging through his mind, they were confused and surprised and shocked. No woman had affected him like Janet's body! The moment she came into his arms she'd been aggressively all over him, unhinged. An explosive fountain of passion that smothered all possible resistance.

It was shockingly overwhelming and wonder-

120

fully pleasing.

Slowly he turned to Janet, reaching his hand to caress the flat of her stomach. He smiled down at her, as she opened her eyes and gazed bright-eyed up at him.

"Oh, I never knew how wonderful it was!" she moaned, her lips rising at the corners. "God, you were good!"

A tremor shuddered through Janet as his fingers slid gently around to her side. Without warning she twisted into his arms, straining against him, moaning, working her hips, caressing his back with her fingertips, locking her legs around his in an attempt to feel more a part of him.

"Again," she whispered in his ear, working it with her lips. "Again! And again, my dear, wonderful lover. I love. Oh, Jim, I love you so much!"

SEX IS MY BUSINESS, BY CHARLES NUETZEL

CHAPTER FIFTEEN

Connie Gales looked across the table at Dale Robbins. For a long time she stared, not speaking, thinking, about Dale and herself. She had had plenty of affairs with men in the past—most of which would be considered cassia; as being cheap tumbles. No affection and no love. But her body had needed men and she had satisfied its urgent hungers.

She had also used her body to help her in business. From the first day she had gone for an interview, Connie had realized that the easy way to good jobs was through sex. Sex had been a good part of her teenage life, and it didn't seem wrong to openly offer to her boss the privilege of exploring her body with his. Why not? And that was the edge she had on other women seeking the same position. Everybody could file, type, and take dictation, or whatever else was required. Not all the ladies were willing to offer other more private duties to their list of required secretarial labors.

But Dale Robbins had different ideas about sex. It was the buildup to romantic affairs and marriage. Marriage, if possible.

"Dale," Connie said in a low whisper, "I wish you would try to understand.

"Understand what?" he snapped, angrily. "I

didn't come here to just understand. Something has to be done about us!

"I can't keep you off my mind—regardless of Haden. There comes a time when reason goes down the crapper—and all a man can do is to try living with things as they are."

"What does *that* mean?"

"Okay—let's start at the beginning. I went out with you because you were attractive. And then we start a light affair—then I discover you are sleeping with Haden...so I'm hurt.

"You finally talk me into coming up to your apartment for dinner. Why I don't really know. We sit here, avoiding the major issue—*us*—and now damn it all we've gotta face it!

"I came here tonight to finally decide how I feel toward you. There is...I can't understand and I can't really forgive—but I could, possibly forget."

Connie's heart jumped. In the past days, since she hadn't been seeing Dale, life had been pretty hard on her. It had been a shock to realize that Dale meant more to her than she had ever imagined. The split had shown that. Now, she was certain he was about to push matters to the limit.

Dale continued: "All I know, Connie, is that I guess...I guess I love you! That's what I've been fighting for days now. And I've come to a point...if I'm right, then it'll be worth it—if I'm wrong...then I've learned a harsh lesson.

"I don't care what you were in the past, or how many men you slept with. What you did in the past made you what you are today—take one experience away from that, and you'd be a different person. I want to marry you—regardless.... What you are

124

now and from now on is all that's important. What do you say?"

For a long time Connie stared at Dale, unable to really believe what she was hearing. She had never thought it was possible for her to take such an offer seriously. Her whole life had been, up to this moment, a strong desire to succeed, as a woman and in the business world; to be self supporting and free from all social limitations. Nothing else had mattered. And she had worked hard to get headed in the right direction.

And now she was willing to give it all up for *one* man? And not a particularly outstanding man— only that she found, silly as it seemed to her, that she loved him. And that was all that mattered.

Most of all that was a real shock.

"The only thing, Connie, you'll have to give up your job. I want a wife who'll be home! Not working!" Dale told her in a firm voice. "I'm old fashioned. I want her to be the mother of my children, a full time mother who can dedicate herself to that … children need both parents being fully involved— and even if it isn't always easy, that's the best solution for a family life. Later, when they're old enough…well, I'm not against a wife working if that's what she wants. What do you say?"

After taking a deep breath, Connie smiled excitedly, and standing, moved around the small table and threw her arms around Dale's neck. "You've got yourself a bargain!"

* * * * * * *

Irene Kilman moved the piece of steak around

on the plate in front of her with a knife, looking nervously up at Henry Kilman.

"Dear...what was it that detective wanted?" she asked her husband.

"Oh, nothing. He's still investigating Bob's death. He believes it might have been murder—not...well, I don't want to talk about it."

Irene flicked her eyes back to the plate and then sighed. "I don't like this idea of Haden going off to the mountains with Janet for the weekend."

"Why?"

"For God's sake, she's your daughter, and you know Jim's reputation with women."

"I also know that he wouldn't do anything wrong. And anyway, Janet is over twenty-one, and much as I hate to think of her going off and letting some fellow play with her body—I couldn't do anything about it even if I wanted to. She's old enough to tell me it's none of my business.

"And, anyway, I don't think she would get involved in a sordid affair. There's nothing wrong with two adults going up to the mountains. And I checked...Haden had reservations for two rooms. Not a double. So...there you are, what's to worry about!"

"They can always go to...oh, to hell with it!"

"Your sudden interest in Janet is a little surprising, Irene," Kilman observed, staring across at her. "It couldn't be that you...find Jim interesting...as a man?"

Irene felt herself tense, and then the oil of sweat covered her skin. She looked fearfully up at her husband.

"Oh, don't look so shocked, Irene," Henry told

126

her, his voice sounding almost amused. "I know all about your little sordid outside activities, and…"

Irene suddenly felt the world explode around her, shattering into a thousand insane pieces, clattering on top of her and making it impossible to breathe. Her mind screamed over and over and over.

God, no!

And what she had done to Bob!

For nothing!

Abruptly her mind retreated inward, closing in on itself until all that was left was blank nothing.

* * * * * * *

The weekend was one series of wonderful caresses; a never ending series that bathed through her whole soul. Once Janet had broken through her mental resistance to having a man make love to her, she felt as if a new world had opened for her, and she wanted to make the most of it as long as it would last.

They left the rooms only a couple of times, once simply to eat dinner, and the second time to have dinner and dance.

James Haden was both gentle and expert. Sometimes when the lovemaking demanded it, he was forceful and almost hurt her, but this was the way she wanted it then; strong and ravishingly overwhelming. It was as if he could read her mind; or as if they were two parts of the same body.

At one point they were in the shower together, and Jim was soaping her body caressingly, sending thrilling stabs of excitement through her every nerve and cell.

"Oh, God, Jim, you're wonderful!" she moaned, pressing herself against him, drawing his body tightly to hers. "Have...have you ever done it in the shower?" she asked, almost frightened that the idea might sound foolish.

But her doubt was short and brief, because Haden moved his hands along her body and then pressed his lips onto hers.

For a long time they clung to each other, and then she felt him suddenly and violently surge to her, and she wanted to scream out in pleasure and agony of it.

Just then there was a sound of banging on the outside door, which led to the hallway.

For a moment Haden froze, and Janet felt a shudder of desperation move through her. That interruption had broken the spell. It had shattered the lusting excitement racing through her body. She looked anxiously at Haden.

The knocking continued.

"A telegram for you, urgent!" a voice called out.

Haden moved away from Janet and then yelled, "Wait a minute—I'll be right there!"

He moved from the shower and after grabbing robe, disappeared from the room. A few moments later he returned, his face white with shock.

"Irene has collapsed! Henry wants us to return right away!"

CHAPTER SIXTEEN

James Haden found the long drive back to town filled with the old depression, but this time it was fuller and more complete. There was a feeling of doom, as if the sudden, unexpected collapse of Irene Kilman marked a new and important element in his own life.

What it could be he didn't know, but there was something in his subconscious mind that cried out a warning. As if a lot of pieces of a picture puzzle had been lying there waiting for the right moment to reveal a half-picture, something his intellect was now able to fill in with logic.

Finally they managed to get back to town. Neither of them had said much during the drive. After having received the telegram, they had packed, paid the bill and then gotten into the car and driven as fast as the speed laws would allow.

Haden wanted to keep from going into the Kilman home, to avoid what he was afraid might happen. There was no reason to be fearful of the next two or three hours, yet he couldn't help or control the inner voice that kept warning him Irene Kilman's condition would have far-reaching effects in his own personal life.

And there was the other feeling, working like an

undercurrent in his emotions, and that concerned Janet. He had used her. The love-making session had been more than he could have wanted, but also confusing.

In those moments in her arms he had almost been able to convince himself he was in love. But love was something, he had learned from past experience, that could be turned on and off. While he was with the woman, he was in love, desperately and completely—if he wanted to be. The moment he left the woman, he could turn it off as one would switch off a radio. It was a state of mind, and nothing more.

Yet, he couldn't get the guilt feelings to subside. What he had done with Janet hadn't been any more or less than what he had done with many women in the past, but this had seemed different. With Janet he felt concern at not being completely honest. He hated the idea of her ever finding out he been lying to her. He also realized that he cared about her feelings for and about him. That was somewhat startling. For normally he didn't give a damn want the woman thought, just so she believed he was a great lover. That was ego. What he felt about Janet was different, deeper, and somewhat frightening.

Even so, Haden realized that all women instinctively knew they would always be taking their chances with men. Women like Janet were always at war with men, and they couldn't help being aware of the gambles involved, especially when they were dealing with their first real affair. This was part of their maturing into well-defined and balanced woman. Growing up could be painful; but necessary in order to survive in the real world.

With Connie Gales it had been different. Goods received in full. Payment for a job. She wanted to get ahead, and had been willing to use sex for the advantages she got in business. He had played it fair with Connie.

With Janet he hadn't played it fair.

Finally he brought his car to a stop in front of the Kilman estate and killed the engine.

"Well, Jan," he said, turning and looking at her. In the darkness, just lightly outlined by a dim moon, Janet's features seemed to be more delicate, more sensual and more desirable than ever before. Maybe it was all in his mind, but he didn't care any more— not about anything.

"Want to go in?" he asked, putting the car key in his pocket.

For a moment Janet didn't say anything, and then, taking a deep breath she turned and looked at Haden.

"I wonder what all the hurry really was all about?"

Haden shrugged and he pulled out a pack of cigarettes.

"Want one?" he offered.

Janet shook her head.

He lighted a cigarette and took a deep drag. It really didn't seem logical that Henry Kilman would have called for them right away—as if it were a matter of life and death.

He decided.

"Come on, let's find out what it's all about!"

Then they were walking into the Kilman home.

"Mr. Kilman is in the den," the butler announced, closing the door behind them.

Without a word the two of them moved down the hall, and then Haden knocked at the huge double doors to the den.

"Yes?" called a tired voice.

"Henry—it's us!"

"Thank God!" Kilman's voice shouted. "Come on in." They opened the doors, stepped in and closed the doors after them.

Henry Kilman was sitting at his huge desk, his face drawn and white, his eyes sunken and his gray hair messed. He looked up at them with a desperate expression.

"I don't know what got into her...just all of a sudden..."

Henry Kilman stared at Jim, a blank expression on his massive face. "We were just talking and then all of a sudden—*bang!* Now she's up in her room. Won't talk to me or anybody!"

Haden stared at Janet, not knowing what to think. There didn't seem any reason for their being sent for, unless Henry had wanted his daughter, had needed her.

"Is there anything I can do?" Haden asked carefully.

"Nothing. I just thought that...maybe Janet should be here with me. I needed someone. Everything happened so fast, I guess I just...panicked."

"Oh, you dear, Father!" Janet rushed to his side and putting her arms around his neck.

Haden sighed and then turned.

"If you need me, I'll be at the apartment," he called, stepping quietly out of the room.

Once in the car, Haden stared blankly at the wheel, trying to settle his jumpy nerves. It seemed all so strange. Everything was too strange.

Why had they been called back? That somehow made him furious inside. At Irene and at Mr. Kilman. Maybe it was simply maddening to have such a wonderful weekend cut short.

No, he realized, *that wasn't it at all!*

The fact was that a sort of magic had developed between Janet and himself up there in the mountains, and he didn't know if it would ever return.

CHAPTER SEVENTEEN

Henry Kilman sat in his den, trying to think out what it was that had bothered his wife. Was it the statement that he knew about her little affairs on the side? But why should that have had such an effect on her?

It didn't seem reasonable. After all, he was a mature man, and he knew the score of life. Young women liked sex, and Irene more than liked it.

He knew it wouldn't be really going too far to say that his wife was bordering on the nymphomaniac.

So, it had been purely normal for her to go out and have her affairs. He wasn't a kid nor as sexually needy as he was years ago. He had actually expected her to have lovers and thought she knew it.

Still, he hadn't told her to take on lovers, in so many words; no matter how broadminded he might be! At least he hadn't until tonight. Well, tacitly he'd said that.

Even though he cared deeply about Irene, he realized she, like any woman, was replaceable. Even if this wasn't what he wanted to do.

Suddenly Henry Kilman wanted to hold her in his arms.

Standing up he moved over to the liquor cabinet

and had a drink. Maybe he should go up and be with Irene. It wasn't the time to caress or kiss, but a time for tenderness. Her sudden breakdown had been a shock.

Henry poured himself a drink, and thought about how the sudden reaction had hit Irene. She had turned pale and white, stood up and clutched her delicate white fingers at her throat. Her eyes had gone wide, and then suddenly she had slipped to the floor.

Henry had rushed to her and tried to revive her. But it hadn't done any good. Quickly he went to the phone and called the family doctor, and after that had sent the telegram to Haden and Janet.

The long wait for the doctor had been a strain on him, because Irene hadn't regained consciousness. He'd gotten her up to her bed with the help of the butler, and then sat at the bedside, waiting.

When the doctor arrived he had quickly managed to bring her around, but she wouldn't talk. She just sat there in bed, staring blankly at them, not speaking, not responding. The doctor had said it was shock. Given her a sedative and then left.

Henry Kilman gulped several swallows of whiskey, then went up to Irene's room.

He opened the door and peeped in. For a moment he thought his eyes were fooling him. That he was seeing things. Then suddenly a choke welled up in his throat and broke out past his heavy lips.

Irene wasn't there.

* * * * * * *

Irene Kilman had been dazed when she felt consciousness returning. For a moment it wasn't possible to figure out where she was. Then slow recognition surfaced. She was lying on her bed. At first she didn't remember what had happened and she didn't know how she had moved to her bedroom. Somebody must have moved her. She had passed out.

Everything rushed back into place with a hammering impact. Feelings of guilt rushed through her like agonizing, stabbing pains her mind couldn't control or stop.

Her whole past life was rushing through her mind like a flashing movie, and the more she tried to stop thinking about it, the worse she felt. Finally she sat up and forced her hands against her face, huge sobs pushing through her body. After a few moments, she stood and stepped to her closet, opening it and picking out a dress. She had to see somebody. Talk to somebody. She had to do something other than be there submerged in inner torment and guilt. Finally dressed, she stepped out of her room and quietly moved down the hall.

She had to talk to somebody who would understand. Somebody who could say, "Okay, you did something bad, and you should be punished for it, but I understand why you did it, and who knows, maybe I would have done the same thing."

That seemed logical enough. Maybe Haden would be a person to see. After all, Haden was a climber and a brutalizing bastard, using women, position and anything he could grab on to in order to make it in his little world! Their world. Of course he'd "understand"! That was only reasonable. It would be insane for him to do otherwise.

She needed to talk to him. He would comfort.

Yes. Of course. That all made sense, her mind argued, confidently. *Do it.*

Anything to hold her sanity together.

Abruptly, Irene realized what she had been planning to do. She returned to her room to wait and think things out a little further. There was time. The idea fascinated her for a moment and then terrified her. But there wasn't anything else she *could* do.

Irene actually laughed at the situation.

But what she needed first was a few drinks, a little boozing to give her strength. Even if the real players might have very few moral ethics. Nobody really gave a damn. It was simply a matter of pointing out the realities to this young man.

She would make things work.

Maybe. Doubt surfaced. Did she have the guts to go through with her plans? Would anybody believe? Could she face the final outcome?

Rational thought teased her: Maybe Haden would be able to suggest an alternative solution, one that would offer escape, and a future.

They could become partners, maybe. They were so alike. Both climbers.

Maybe there was an alternative.

She hoped so. She had to get his help. She needed a skillful, sharp mind to help her sort things out.

After all, that was the only sane thing to do.

A few nice shots to focus her mind, then to Haden's apartment. She *had* to talk to him.

Silently, Irene moved down the steps and then along the hall and after that outside. Walking along the path to her car, which was in the garage, Irene slipped into the night.

CHAPTER EIGHTEEN

James Haden lay in a half-sleep, half-dreaming about the wonderful feel of Janet's body against his. Only because he was slightly plastered, was he able to think about Janet without depression.

In that cloudy state, he could dream and feel and experience mentally the physical sensations of Janet and her love-making. It was almost unbelievable to realize that Janet had been holding back all that wonderful, delightful talent all these years!

She was obviously in love with him. That was the only thing that made sense, the only rational explanation.

Sound jarred his mental world.

Haden tried to move, but his body was too relaxed, still caught up in the half-sleep.

It was knocking. A pounding.

Vaguely he wondered why it was important that he should get up.

The knocking sounded from the front door.

"Jim Haden!" a woman's voice called desperately.

He couldn't make out who it was. But it could only be one person, Haden thought dreamily.

Janet Kilman.

"Wait!" he finally managed to shout back.

Abruptly, he commanded his body and it rose from the bed, and then Haden stepped across the room to the front door. He was still fully clothed, having come home and immediately started drinking, then flopped on his bed.

Anxiously he swung open the door, trying to focus his blurry eyes. For a moment he swayed dizzily.

For a moment he stood there, forcing his eyes open, and then they came to focus on a dark red skirt. The curves were lovely and rounded, full and voluptuous.

This wasn't Janet! Janet was smaller!

Shock jolted Haden's mind for a moment and he straightened up and gazed at...

Irene Kilman!

"Swat the shell you doing here?" he demanded in a slurring voice. "Sham it all!"

Angrily he tried to gain control of his tongue.

"Close the door," Irene commanded. Then she stepped into the room and closed it. "I had to see you...had to see somebody!"

Suddenly, Haden remembered that Irene was supposed to be ill in her room at the Kilman mansion. What was she doing here?

"What you doing here?"

"You have a drink?" she requested, searching the room.

"A bottle...shin...on the floor. By the bed."

Slowly Haden's speech was regaining its normal pitch and control. The drinks and the sleep had dulled his tongue, but the shock of seeing Irene Kilman in his apartment jarred his mind into slowly waking from the dull half-sleep.

140

It took Irene Kilman several moments to find the bottle. It was half empty. She just raised the bottle to her lips and started gulping.

Haden stared at her, shocked.

"What you come here for?" Haden finally managed to ask in a controlled and even voice. He seated himself on a chair and gazed at Irene. He couldn't help admitting to himself that she was a beautiful woman; more than just attractive—she was stunning.

Irene ignored him for a long while, her full attention centered on the bottle. Her face was drawn and pale. Her eyes were deep and dark. There was a half hysterical expression on her features—nothing that Haden could really label or point to; it was more like a projected inner feeling which her features were radiating. And in that was a slight edge of...near madness.

It was the way a person might look if they had seen a dead person walking. Shock and a little terror.

Irene gulped the whiskey again and then sat waiting, as if taking in every numbing sensation of the liquor.

"What is it you want?" Haden demanded, slowly beginning to feel a little irritation.. Irene Kilman had already caused him enough trouble; actually she had seduced him. He didn't want to get more involved with her than he already was.

Now, here she was, in his apartment, wanting something—and he wasn't sure he was about to give her *anything.*

"Shut up!" Irene finally said, gulping on the bottle again. She abruptly looked at him and a sneer spread across her red lips.

"You and me...we're alike! You and me. We..." She turned her attention back to the bottle.

There was a long silence, and the Irene gazed up again at Haden. She smiled for a moment and then her eyes widened in sheer horror.

"Oh, God! What kind of people are we? The social climbers! If somebody gets in our way—crush them like a bug!

"We don't care what happens to others, as long as *we* get what we want. But believe me...it catches up with you! It gets you where it hurts—and then finally it twists around your life until there isn't any breath left in you.

"You..." Irene paused, puzzled and startled at what she was saying. "I don't know why I'm telling you this," she choked out, in a heavy sob. For a moment her features struggled, and then finally taking a deep breath, she announced:

"That's not true. I had to talk to somebody like myself. Somebody who might understand what motives caused me to...Oh, God!"

The bottle dropped from her fingers and clattered like a bomb on the floor. Her hands went up to her face, covering her eyes and mouth. A deep, agonized sob shook her frame.

Haden looked at her, stunned. First her words and now this. He didn't know if he felt sorry for her or not. But one thing he did know was that he didn't have the vaguest idea what she was talking about. Yet, what she had said was true. She was talking about him, too.

People like himself and Irene and Connie Gales would crush anything that got in their way. Or al-

142

most anything. They would struggle, selling them-selves out to the highest bidder, doing anything to get ahead. Not caring who got hurt.

That was what bothered Haden. He was doing this to Janet, and that's why he had come home and gotten plastered, not caring about anything but es-cape. Maybe that *was* a slim difference between Irene Kilman and himself. She had sold out. Haden was aware of Irene's speaking again.

"I was just a small town kid who got a lot of bad breaks. My father drank too much—to his death. My mother died when I was only fifteen. I lived with my aunt...ran away when I was nineteen and I've been determined to make a good go at it ever since then. All my family was poor—so to be-come a success I had to make money—or marry into money. Boy—how I worked! I really worked hard!" A choke sobbed in her throat, and for a moment she looked down at the floor.

"Why are you telling me this?" Haden asked, feeling uneasy. She shouldn't be telling him her life history. Even if he were interested. He had problems of his own—yet, just for human decency, he couldn't deny her right to have a silent ear to tell her troubles to.

Irene gazed up at Haden for a moment. She looked more serious, more rational, and then said: "I'm going to the police after I talk to you."

"What?"

"I'll tell you in good time," she answered in a shaky voice. Her hands were clutched together, tightly, working nervously, the fingers almost seem-ing to shake, as they intertwined.

Haden felt the need for a drink and went into the

kitchen to get another bottle of whiskey. He returned, two glasses filled with whiskey. One he handed to Irene Kilman, who looked up into his eyes, thanking him.

"Jim, you know what it is like to want something, and go out and get it—I know, because we're two of a kind. We both are after the same things—Only I made a big mistake!"

"What kind of mistake did you make, Irene," Haden wanted to know.

"A very large one." Irene stared at him, and then taking a deep breath she said, "Let's go easy first. I'll tell you the whole thing in a slow way, so that maybe you'll understand—for I'm going to have to have understanding."

Irene took a large swallow from her drink and then stared into the glass. "Like I was telling you. Life wasn't easy, and so I just started out, sleeping my way up. I found out quick enough that I liked sex—liked it a lot, and so I didn't find it too hard to get ahead.

"I learned all the tricks on how to please a man, and the ways to make him want more. That's the secret—you know. A woman who simply gives her body might find herself out in the street in a couple of hours, with no job and only her little affair to show for the efforts. The secret is to make the man like it, so he'll want to come back for more.

"I got to be good at that!"

She took another swallow of her drink, and then continued. "So I came to this hole of a town and got a job with Kilman Enterprises—and made Henry. It wasn't so hard. In fact it was quite easy. He was lonely and...even though he couldn't possibly satisfy

144

me at his age—and for that matter, I discovered earlier in life that no man can satisfy me...I need sex a lot more than most women.

"Anyway, I went out to get him and all his money, and after that I just went on taking other lovers on the side. I thought I was being pretty careful and clever. Then suddenly Bob Kilman discovered what was going on and threatened to go tell Henry.

"And..."

Irene broke off, a terrified expression squeezing her pretty features. Then after taking a large gulp of the whiskey, she said: "Well, can't you see that there wasn't anything else I *could* do?"

Haden felt a gripping in his chest, his whole body tensed.

Irene's voice was shaking as she said: "I had to kill him—it was the only thing I could do! I had to save my position...but...oh, God!"

CHAPTER NINETEEN

The room at the police station was quiet and. Haden was sitting in a chair across from Janet, trying hard not to look at her. Henry Kilman was sitting white-faced. They had been waiting a long time for Irene Kilman's statement to the police to be completed.

Janet sighed and then turned her eyes toward Haden.

"I just can't believe it," she said in a dazed voice.

It was the first words that had been spoken, except for a quick explanation made over the phone to Henry Kilman, about an hour before, that Haden was taking Irene down to the police.

When they had all arrived at the station, Henry had simply asked: "What's this all about?"

Haden had answered, "Irene wants to tell the police about how she killed Bob." They had sat still after that, everybody too exhausted emotionally to say anything.

"How'd it happen?" Henry Kilman finally asked, gazing across at Haden, his eyes dead and dull, his thick lips drooping.

"When you told her tonight that you knew about the little affairs she'd been carrying on, on the side, she cracked. That's all. The strain of what she had done had finally gotten through to her in one explosion. After that, she knew there was only one thing that she could do. But first she wanted to talk to somebody like me...so..."

"How'd she do it—why?"

"It wasn't so difficult," Haden told him in a flat, unemotional voice. "She found out that Bob was going to tell you, and she saw her whole future exploding—all her well worked-out plans, and she decided there was nothing else to do but stop him from talking to you. She took him up to her room—and made love to Bob."

"Oh, God, no!" Janet cried out.

Haden was just about to finish when Lieutenant Brown stepped into the room. His face was drawn and tired looking, but he managed to smile as he stepped up to Henry Kilman.

"I don't know exactly how to tell you this, Henry," he said.

"I know," Kilman stated, standing and looking grimly at the police officer. "Irene killed Bob." His voice was heavy and bitter sounding. "And I thought I knew her..."

Lieutenant Brown showed no signs of shock. "I'm afraid you're all...well, Irene *thinks* she killed your son. That's not quite true. She seems to have been responsible for his death, but she didn't actually kill. him. He *did* kill himself. I must admit I was a little confused about the whole thing. I believed he had been murdered—but from what Irene has told me..."

Brown broke off suddenly and then said: "I've called Doctor Turner. He'll be over to see Irene—

the shock of everything has been a strain on her emotions. I'm afraid she's going to need professional help."

Haden tensed, surprised. "What are you talking about."

"Well, you see, from everything I've been able to find out about Bob Kilman's death—supported by what Mrs. Kilman said—he *did* shoot himself, because of the fact that he'd had an affair with his stepmother."

Suddenly Haden felt a sickness inside his guts. Everything seemed to rush through his whole being—all the events of the past days. He had walked through the last couple of hours in a daze, brought on both by the liquor and what Irene Kilman had said to him.

Now, suddenly it all shook through him and all he wanted to do was run—run and never stop running.

Run from himself, run from everything that he had made of his life. It all seemed terrible—all the events and all the things he had done to get himself ahead in life. And the seducing of Janet, and now this new added fact of what a woman—much like himself in many ways—had done to a damned nice guy!

Without knowing what he was doing, Haden suddenly found himself rushing from the police station. Abruptly he was aware of standing outside the huge building, on the sidewalk. It was Janet's voice that brought him out of the shock.

"Jim—wait!"

Janet was the last person in the world he wanted to talk to, or be with. Yet there was something that held him frozen. He didn't move.

"Jim, what are you doing?" Janet asked, moving around in front of him and gazing up into his eyes. There was concern lining her features. Her eyes were moist and her face a little flushed.

"Janet—just leave me. I have to be alone!"

"What's wrong?"

For a moment Haden stared at her and then made a sudden decision. He couldn't do to Janet what Irene had done to Bob. He would ruin her life if he let it go on any longer. Taking a deep breath, Haden reached out and took hold of Janet's shoulders, squeezing hard. She cringed at the pressure of his touch, but didn't say anything.

"Don't you *understand?*" he demanded, nastily; as cruelly as he could make his voice sound.

"What?" All her innocence was in Janet's voice. "Whatever it is, I want to help. A person in love wants to help the one that loves them!"

Haden laughed bitterly. "I don't love you! I was just using you. That's all. Just like Irene used your Dad. I wanted to marry you for your money. That's all!"

For a moment Janet stared blankly at Haden, and then her lower lip started to tremble and her eyes reddened, as tears slowly began streaming down her cheeks.

"So—get out of my life, before I ruin you, too!"

Haden roughly pushed Janet away from him and then moved hurriedly to his car, got in and started the engine. Gunning the gas pedal, he charged the car down the street.

* * * * * * *

Janet Kilman stood on the sidewalk, staring at Haden's retreating car, stunned by his words, unable to think for a long time. She didn't know how long she stood there before she started walking. She wasn't aware that she was walking.

First it was the numbing sting of hurt pride, and the realization of what a fool she had been. *How could she let herself be taken in by the oldest line in the world.*

She walked for a long time and her mind started thinking along other lines, other than personal hurt pride.

One question caused her to change things completely for her.

Why had Jim told her those horrible things?

What followed was a series of questions that piled together into a major puzzle that didn't fit his outburst.

She realized he had nothing to gain by having said those things. He could have continued to play the game, being the understanding friend and lover. That was what she would have wanted. And it wouldn't have been long before they would have married. The idea of being Haden's wife was more than appealing. If only he really loved her! If only things had been different.

SEX IS MY BUSINESS, BY CHARLES NUETZEL

CHAPTER TWENTY

Haden sat in his room, gulping whiskey. He didn't know how long he had been there, for time had blended into a blur, and all he knew was that everything that he had worked so hard for stopped existing. For one moment of noble insanity, he had crushed everything he had sweated for and planned to take.

Now, even if he wanted to, it would be impossible to have Janet. In that one instant when he had been under shock and under depression, he had blown the whole thing into a million worthless pieces. He was finished. Done. Ended. The whole thing was over.

And yet, he couldn't feel he had done the wrong thing with Janet. Ever since he had started out to seduce her, quickly, because of the pressure from Gordon Fuller, he had felt a terrible sense of guilt and depression. He hadn't been able to get it out of his system. He was a bastard and he knew it.

So now maybe he wasn't such a bastard anymore. He'd ruined everything. All he could do was pack up and leave town, start all over again. Maybe this time he would go about things differently.

A pang went suddenly through him.

He wouldn't be able to make love to Janet

again. Never know the thrill of being near her, holding her, caressing her, kissing her. More than that.

Suddenly he really wanted to be with this woman he had magically bonded to.

And far too late to do anything about.

He'd found a heavenly paradise with Janet in that hotel room they had shared together for two long nights and one long day.

Finished, now. Never to be captured.

Haden wished he had waited a little longer before letting Janet know the truth. He could have taken her someplace and made love to her once more.

That word, love, suddenly stopped Haden.

But only for a moment. He changed it to sexual relations.

Yes, he thought, *that was much better!*

But why should it have bothered him? It didn't seem reasonable.

Angrily, Haden reached for the bottle and poured himself a strong drink. For a long time he just stared at the brownish, golden liquid, not moving, contemplating it. One more drink would mean slow blackout. He'd had enough, already. His head felt like a tight band had been pressed around it, giving off a soothing, numbing effect that dulled the world around him and focused his inner thoughts into strong awareness.

All he wanted to do was escape from the total defeat his life had become.

At least he still had a job.

* * * * * * *

154

Janet Kilman's mind was beginning to get fuzzy, confused, as she started back to the house. She had somehow returned home, gotten her car and was driving aimlessly. Her mind was still spinning over and over, around and around, agonizingly.

Why had Jim told her those horrible things? If he hadn't, she would never have known the truth, and what she hadn't known wouldn't really have hurt her...

What was wrong with her? Didn't she have any pride? Didn't she care about anything...?

Oh, how she loved Jim Haden!

Why, oh, why had he told her?

Abruptly she tensed, dazed by a sudden realization. The realization had come when she attempted to answer that question.

There hadn't been any reason for Haden to tell her! He had everything to lose. Everything that he had so skillfully worked and planned and developed.

There was only one answer that was logical.

Haden really loved her and he didn't know it! Haden had told her that because he didn't want to hurt her any further. He *had* to be in love to do that!

Sudden excitement flooded through Janet, like a torrent of loving ecstasy.

There just couldn't be any other reason for Haden to have revealed to her that he didn't love her—that he had used her—unless he *was* in love. He had given up everything—and he didn't really know why, himself!

All at once, Janet realized what she had to do. She had to find Haden and make him accept the truth, too. She had to convince him he was just running away from himself and not from her. And not for the reasons he thought.

She had to find Haden, before it was too late.

* * * * * * *

Vaguely, Haden was aware of knocking taking place somewhere in the world outside his mind. For a long time he couldn't make out from where, then suddenly he was jolted by the fact that it was coming from his front door. Somebody was outside in the hall, knocking on his door.

Who?

It couldn't be Irene this time.

Haden looked at his watch. It took a couple of seconds to focus on the little numbers and the hands.

It was three-ten. Who would be wanting to see him this time of the morning? Had Janet Kilman told her father, and did the old man want to put Haden in his place?

Panic bolted through him. He tensed and felt an aching pain in every muscle. What was he going to do?

Then suddenly he hardened inside. If it was Henry Kilman even that game would be shattered.

He was a bastard and deserved anything that anybody would want to give him, especially from Janet's father.

Tiredly, with effort, Haden stood and moved toward the door. For a moment he stood there, almost out a shaky hand toward the knob and turned it. A moment later he was looking into the features of Janet Kilman.

For a long, stunned moment he couldn't say anything. There wasn't a reason in the world he could think of for her being there—unless she had come to kill him. But then, his dazed mind reasoned: maybe that was what he deserved. To hell with everything!

Then another emotion flooded into him.

Dear Janet! Beautiful, desirable Janet. Sexy Janet. Wonderful, delightful Janet!

Angrily he forced the thoughts down into a pit in his mind.

"What are you doing here?" he demanded in a hard voice.

Janet smiled and then asked: "Can't I come in?"

"What for?"

She ignored him and stepped into the room.

"Close the door," she told him.

"What the hell?"

"Close the door!" she demanded. Then she smiled, almost tenderly.

In a daze, Haden closed the door, slowly.

"I wanted to talk to you, Jim," Janet announced.

"I don't see what we have to talk about," he snapped, moving over to the table where his half empty glass of whiskey was sitting.

Janet moved faster, coming between him and the liquor. "No more drinks—not right now!"

"What the hell?"

"I want to talk to you about something. I want to have my say and then you can do what you want!"

There was a strange firmness in Janet's voice that stopped Haden. And there was something else mixed with it—something he couldn't quite place, right then.

"What do you want?"

"To ask you a simple question'

"What?"

"Why did you tell me what you did last night?"

For a moment Haden gazed *at* her, then he said:

"Because I didn't want to hurt you any more!"

"Why not?"

"What do you mean by that?" he demanded, feeling a nervous grind *at* the pit of his guts.

"Just answer the question!" she ordered in a firm voice, her face set and expressionless.

For a long while, Haden thought that over. Why had he not wanted to hurt her? Because she was too nice a girl to be hurt. But why should that matter to him? Angrily, he said. "I don't know, and I don't care!"

Janet grinned, almost tenderly.

"I think you *do* care," she announced in a soft voice. "I think that's the reason you told me. Because you *are* in love with me!"

Haden felt his whole body tingle. It was as if everything had drained from him. It didn't seem possible, after what he had told Janet, that she could come back and say what she had—unless for revenge.

"Are you kidding?"

"Not at all. It's the only reason I can think of." For a moment Janet paused, her lips half parted, her eyes wide and innocent looking.

"I want you to think that over!" Then she stepped aside and started for the door.

All of a sudden, Haden saw what was really going on. Janet was so much in love with him that she was willing to sell herself for the chance of getting

158

him back. It didn't seem possible. Yet, now he was being offered a second chance, and if he played the game right, he could have her, and the job and the money and everything.

All the social standing he had wanted and worked to get! He could, very easily, convince her to marry him. It didn't seem possible—but there it was.

"Wait!" he shouted, aware that even the liquor effects had slipped away for the most part, because of this sudden shock; this second chance.

Janet paused and turned and looked at him. "What?"

In a split second Haden thought out his next move. Moving forward, he took Janet into his arms. She didn't resist, but, instead, pressed eagerly and anxiously against him.

"I guess you were right," he managed to force himself to say.

As they kissed passionately, Haden felt an excitement move through his whole being. Without knowing how it had happened, the magic of the weekend in the mountains was returning with the excitement of this one embrace.

"Oh, God, Jim, I love you!" Janet moaned in his ear.

Haden knew what Janet wanted. It was as if he could read her mind. Without a word he lifted her into his arms and carried her across to the entrance to his bedroom. A moment later he laid her down on the bed.

Janet smiled up at him. She looked so beautiful and loveable! So delightful and innocent.

Haden gazed down at her and suddenly was

stunned by an overwhelming emotion. An emotion he wasn't used to, and that scared him, he wanted to rebel from it.

But that was impossible. There was nothing he could do about the feeling, because it flooded through him like an all-powerful force. He had no control over anything.

Questions dazed him, battling against his resistance, demanding answers he didn't want to give.

Janet's question: *Why had he told her he had been using her?*

And if it was because he didn't want to hurt her—*was* it because he really loved her?

That statement shocked him, but not as much as he would have thought. Here was his chance. But was he just fooling himself? Was he just trying to find a reason to talk himself into thinking he was in love with Janet?

Janet was a thoughtful, forgiving, nice young girl, who had a lot to give a man—more than any other woman he had known. There wasn't any reason why he couldn't have fallen in love with her, without even knowing it. The fact that he'd destroyed all his chances for the social position he had wanted so badly, seemed to imply he *had* been motivate by love.

"What's keeping you, Jim?" Janet asked, raising her arms toward him.

Haden smiled and then slid down next to Janet. Just before their lips touched, he took a deep breath and then asked the only question possible for him to ask: "Janet, would you go away with me—away from this town, to build our own lives, by ourselves? Without any Kilman influences?"

160

"Without dad's influence, power, position?" Janet inquired, puzzled sounding.

The question surprised even him, but it was the only way for Haden to prove to himself that he really loved Janet.

She smiled at him and said in a soft voice, "Anything you want, dear. If that's what it takes to get you."

As their lips met, Haden realized the truth about himself and his feelings for Janet. Sometime, somewhere, somehow, he had, unknowingly, really fallen in love with Janet—and all at once he was happy about it; happier than he had ever been in his whole life.

Suddenly there seemed a real reason to live.

But for the next couple of hours Haden didn't think about that any more. He was too much in love, and too busy proving it to his future wife.

Later they would decide where their future might take them. Right now they simply had one another and their mutual commitment to love one another.

And, strangely enough, that's all that counted.

ABOUT THE AUTHOR

Charles Nuetzel was born in San Francisco in 1934, and writes:

"As long as I can remember I wanted to be a writer. It was a dream I never thought would materialize. But with the help of Forrest J Ackerman, who became my agent, I managed to finally make it into print.

"I was lucky enough not only in selling my work to publishers but also ending up packaging books for some of them, and finally becoming a 'publisher' much like those who had bought my first novels. From there it as a simple leap to editing not only a science-fiction anthology, but also a line of SF books for Powell Sci-Fi back in the 1960s. Throughout these active professional years I had the chance to design some covers and do graphic cover layouts for pocket books & magazines."

Much of his work in covers and graphics are a result of having had a father who was a professional commercial artist, and who did a number of covers for sci-fi magazines in the 1950s and later for pocket books—even for some of Mr. Nuetzel's books.

In retirement he has become involved in swing dancing, a long time lover of Big Band jazz. But more interestingly world travels have taken him (and his wife Brigitte) across the world, to Hawaii, Caribbean, Mexico, Kenya, Egypt, Peru, having a lifelong interest in ancient civilizations. His website is full of thousands of pictures taken during these trips.